MASADA

The author is fascinated by the early civilisations and how they were created, additionally by the way that some civilisations have persecuted the beliefs of others, often causing unjust persecution and genocide. His story of mankind's domination of the world, often depicts the inadequacies of this form of control, which so often causes hardship and cruelty realise that it is very difficult to suggest an amicable compromise, but I sincerely believe that we may one day achieve a realistic goal, that allows different beliefs to exist in harmony.

Published Work:

If Only They Knew (2008)
Olympia Publishers
ISBN: 978 1905513 37 6

MASADA

Peter Cordwell

MASADA

Olympia Publishers
London

www.olympiapublishers.com

OLYMPIA PAPERBACK EDITION

A CIP catalogue record for this title is
available from the British Library.

ISBN: 978-1-905513-94-9

This is a work of fiction.
Names, characters, places and incidents originate from the writer's
imagination. Any resemblance to actual persons, living or dead, is purely
coincidental.

Cover design by BRONOWSKI ©2009

First Published in 2009

Olympia Publishers part of Ashwell Publishing Ltd
60 Cannon Street
London
EC4N 6NP

Printed in Great Britain

I would like to dedicate this book to my father,
Dennis Cordwell,
who has always been an inspiration in my life.

I would like to thank my carers, who were chosen for their typing and reading skills, as I am registered blind and also very difficult to understand.

Fortunately my disability does not affect my brain-power, for which I have written many other books featuring many of the ancient wonders of the world.

Part One

"Gladiator to Centurion"

The two opponents circled each other, each carefully watching the others eyes that would betray a sudden attack. Both men were bleeding now and the fight was at least twenty minutes old, judging by the water clock. Their wounds were only superficial, although they bled profusely. Both men were well muscled and very efficient at the job of killing their adversary. The sun blazed down out of the light blue sky in northwest Gaul on a warm spring afternoon. One of the contestants was a black man from Africa, he was slightly taller than the white man and he was deadly with the net and trident. His opponent was a Briton, captured when fishing by General Priam when he sighted the large invasion fleet while aboard his fishing boat. That was six years ago now and he had just stared in his small fishing boat and gaped at the huge galley, not even realising what it was. He was only seventeen summers old when he was taken. Now, he had worked hard, training as a gladiator using the sword and small round shield. His wounds were from the prongs of the trident that Adobe, the African, had sharpened with a file and stone until their arrowheads were as sharp as a razor. The Briton was not quite as tall, but equally well muscled. His name was Hugh and he had made only one lunge so far which had just caught the African on the side of his chest as he twisted away. The African had a shallow cut across his chest that had been made by a swipe he had only narrowly avoided by leaping back. The two men were normally friends, but had been chosen to fight by Aurolius, the owner of the Gladiators. He had selected his finest pair for the fight, to impress General Priam and Senator Latitch who were his guests.

Hugh was thinking about his capture, but kept his eyes fixed on the dark brown eyes of Adobe, as he knew that a fleeting lack of concentration would be all that Adobe needed to ensnare him with the net and then finish him off with the trident. It was as if General Priam had read Hugh's thoughts, for he leaned closer in to watch the fight and see how Hugh managed to avoid the probing trident which had already caused shallow grazes to Hugh's shoulder and his left leg. Most gladiator fights would have been over in half the time that these two had been fighting, but neither of these two showed any sign of weakness and Aurolius wanted to create a good impression especially in front of the Roman Senator. As General Priam moved closer, the African seemed to slip, although he was barefooted and the arena was hard sand. Hugh moved in for the killing thrust, only to realise that he had been outwitted. The black man had not slipped, but twisted aside and cast the net, which now wrapped itself around Hugh. He was completely entangled in the net and could only hope for mercy. Before Adobe ended the fight with a clean thrust of his trident, he looked up at the small crowd of watchers. Normally when gladiators have fought well, they receive the thumbs up signal, allowing their opponents to go free. Aurolius glanced at Senator Latitch who gave the thumbs down signal. Although Hugh had fought bravely he was fighting at a disadvantage, as Adobe was a master with the net and trident, which nearly always won against the sword and shield. Adobe was incensed by the injustice of the decision and rather than finish his friend, he whirled around and threw the trident at the Senator. The throw would have skewered the Senator, but General Priam acted quickly. He kicked the chair that the Senator was sitting on, so that he landed in an untidy heap on the floor, as the trident whistled over his head and slammed into the woodwork behind where the Senator had been sitting. The enraged Adobe launched himself at the watchers box where one of the soldiers on guard duty hurled his javelin at the African's back. Even this did not stop the African as he tried to reach the Senator, who was now being helped to his feet by his two bodyguards. The African was trying to haul himself into the box despite the javelin still hanging from his back. General Priam stood up and grabbed the African's hair and forced his head forward and cut down through the African's spinal cord with his dagger. The black man collapsed back into the arena completely lifeless.

"I think we have seen enough blood shed today, Aurolius," said General Priam.

"I think we can let the other gladiator go free, as he fought well."

Aurolius led the small group of spectators from the box. As General Priam was leaving he gave a small nod of recognition and of gratitude to Hugh for having fought a spectacular fight. The soldiers helped to unravel Hugh from the net and led him out of the arena to where the doctor could tend his wounds. The doctor was very experienced in dealing with gladiator wounds and already had a hot bowl of water, into which he poured some strong smelling liquid. He washed Hugh's injured arm first and said, "None of these wounds are deep and the liquid that I have just put in the water will sting but will stop the wounds from mortifying and from becoming infected."

"Ouch!" exclaimed Hugh, as the doctor washed him. The doctor quickly bandaged his arm from wrist to elbow before turning to the shallow cut in Hugh's side. Hugh winced as the doctor cleaned up the cut and bandaged it tightly, telling Hugh that he was a real child, as he made so much fuss over his injuries. When the doctor had finished he ushered Hugh into the room behind him that was the room normally left for the winner of a gladiators contest, much to Hugh's surprise. But when he came to think about it, it was obvious that there was only going to be one survivor. The more Hugh thought about it, he realised that the exhibition was for Senator Latitch, who had condemned him, yet Adobe had not killed him and was grateful to General Priam, who had stopped his soldiers from killing Hugh in the first place. He had been sold to Aurolius, as Priam had noticed the boy's strength and possibility as a gladiator. Hugh felt his hatred of the weak chinned Senator, and now realised why he was called the Hangman's Dilemma, as he effectively had no chin. Although he did not realise it at the time, Hugh would have a lot to do with the evil Senator later. He sat on the low couch that was the room's only furniture, when the other door to the small room opened and the girl came in. She was possibly a couple of years younger than Hugh, but she had caught his eye more than once, when serving the gladiators after a training session. She was a typical dark haired Frankish beauty and was undoubtedly there as a reward. She loosened the cord around her neck, which allowed the simple dress to fall to the floor, revealing that she wore nothing underneath. As she stepped forward into Hugh's embrace, he noticed that her clear green eyes were not entirely green, but basically green, yet shot through with golden highlights that simply added to her beauty.

After Hugh and the girl had satisfied their carnal desires, they fell asleep in each other's arms. When Hugh awoke a short while later he found that she was awake and studying his face, taking in his hazel coloured eyes and dark brown hair that Hugh often described as the colour of dark mud.

"I am glad that you were my reward, but I still don't know your name, although I think you know that I am called Hugh," he enquired.

"Yes Hugh, I too am glad that I was chosen and that you were the winner. My name is Rosanna," she informed him.

He then told her that he had not really been the victor of the fight, but that Adobe had really beaten him. He gave her all the details of the fight and said that he was fortunate to be alive. He told her that everything had been simply a display for Senator Latitch and he and Adobe had become close friends. Adobe was beginning to teach him the language of the Forests, from where he came in Africa, hoping that they would go back there one day as friends. As he told her this, he realised that there were tears in his eyes, these he cuffed away angrily.

She then told him about herself and that she had been originally a free woman, but was captured a few years ago from the north of Gaul, where the Roman Legions were still held in check. She went on to explain about her work in the kitchens, from where she had often been serving the food to the gladiators when they had finished their training.

As there seemed to be no rush, they made love again this time more slowly and with far more passion, after which they slept again. They awoke just as the sun was turning the sky light, yet there were only sounds of movement in the gladiator training arena. Rosanna decided that she had better dress and return to her work. She had just left and as Hugh fastened his tunic around his waist, one of the doors opened and one of the guards told him that General Priam wished to speak with him. The soldier then ushered Hugh through the door and slipped out as the General entered.

"You fought bravely yesterday," said the General.

"Thank you General, it is a long time since you captured me. How is the conquest of Britain progressing?"

"Very well Hugh, we have established a base on one of their larger rivers, they call it Londonium.

"However, I have come here to discuss another matter with you. You see we have vacancies for new soldiers, we are now allowed to recruit from the countries that we have now occupied, instead of waiting for trainees to be sent from Rome. Therefore I have come to offer you a position as one of my new soldiers, you will receive the standard pay and become a free man." He stood waiting for Hugh's reply.

Hugh waited quite a while before he replied, as he was doing some quick thinking. He realised that the General had used his influence over Aurolius and he wanted to work for this considerate General, who was brave yet kind.

"I would like very much to be a soldier in one of your legions sir, but would I be allowed to take my woman with me."

"You realise that I will have to buy her from Aurolius?"

"Yes sir, I realise that," replied Hugh.

"Alright Hugh, but I will expect you to work hard for me." He then turned and left Hugh alone.

Hugh left the chamber and went back to where the gladiators were training, simply hoping that General Priam would be able to negotiate Rosanna's release for him to take as his woman. Hugh was just talking to one of the gladiator trainers about how soon he could take off the bandages. He turned around at the mention of his name, to see General Priam and Aurolius coming over towards him. "We have some good news for you Hugh," said Aurolius, "as you fought a very spectacular battle with Adobe, who is now dead, for which I am sorry, as apart from being a close friend of yours, he was one of my best gladiators." Hugh made a gesture and was about to speak, but Aurolius waved his gesture aside and said, "I had a question asking if you could take Rosanna with you, particularly as Senator Latitch has returned to Rome." Hugh stood in complete amazement, he just gazed in wonder at the General. Priam was not as tall as Hugh, but of average height, very broad and someone who exuded confidence, he was the sort of man you trusted on first sight. It took him a moment to realise that Aurolius was speaking once again.

"I will leave the general to explain, as you and Rosanna are now under his command." With that Aurolius left him with the General.

General Priam looked at Hugh before saying, "Aurolius was quite happy about letting Rosanna go with you, although soldiers' wives are allowed to come with their legions when they are not on campaign. At the moment the main legion under my command is the 9th and we are waiting for instructions. I believe that we may be sailing back to Britain where you came from, so your knowledge of the language will be an advantage. For the time being if you collect Rosanna from the kitchen and meet me in a short while, I suggest you wait by the gate where I will meet you soon and take you to where we are permanently based. He left Hugh fairly satisfied, that everything had been organised so efficiently. Hugh stood staring after the general and soon he realised that he had better go and find Rosanna in the kitchen and tell her the good news. He found her sooner than he thought and was pleased to know that she had already been informed and needed very little time to get ready and come with him. She took his hand in hers and as she squeezed his hand she leant near to him.

"Thank you Hugh for taking me with you, it is what I really wanted. Does this mean that I will become your wife?"

"I suppose it does," he replied. "Although I do not know exactly what the Roman law is, but you are definitely my woman, so I suppose we will have to ask General Priam what the exact procedure is." They soon reached the gates and waited until General Priam came along accompanied by two of his centurions.

As the General approached, he said to Hugh, "So this is your woman, Hugh?" He gave an appraising glance at Rosanna and introduced Hugh to his two centurions. "This is Rolex and you will be under his command during your training, and don't think that you do not need training, because if you are already a good fighter, you see, being a soldier who is not just fighting in single combat, the entire strategy is different. That is what the other centurion will be teaching you." Here he indicated to the other centurion with him, "This is Crelux and he will teach you about the strategy of fighting in the army, which is very different and will even take you a while to get used to it. Now let me walk with Rosanna, whilst you walk with Rolex and Crelux. I am sure that Rosanna wants to ask me about where you will be staying and what I have in mind for her."

As General Priam walked in front with Rosanna, Hugh walked behind, between the two centurions, noticing as he did so that both of them were shorter than he was. He spoke to his new commander, Centurion Rolex, "As you are my new Commanding Officer, can you give me details where we will be staying and for how long?"

Rolex was of either Roman or Greek descent and he spoke with a definite accent that Hugh thought he recognised as Greek, because one of his fellow gladiators had been Greek. "Alright Hugh, we are temporarily based about three miles from here, and mainly everybody sleeps under canvas, although I am not sure where the General intends you to sleep tonight, as we have no spare sleeping quarters." He quickly added as an after thought, "Well certainly not for married couples."

Crelux leered at Hugh and said, "Needless to say you want to sleep with your pretty wife tonight." He gave an evil grin, exposing broken and discoloured teeth. Hugh instantly took a dislike to Crelux, but was careful not to let his feeling show on his expression, for he knew that if this man was going to be his Commander in weapon trading, he should show respect, certainly until he knew the man's weakness, even though he thought to himself that he would exploit the weakness later. He simply smiled back at Crelux, as if sharing the jest. They walked behind General Priam who was deep in conversation with Rosanna for most of the way, keeping a respectful gap between themselves and the General, so that his conversation with Rosanna was not overheard, although Hugh knew that he would hear anything of interest from Rosanna later on. Hugh tried to keep his stride exactly the same as Rolex and Crelux, even though the sight of marching men had at first amused him, because the British tribes had never marched in step before, but this discipline obviously had made the Roman Empire so great. He believed it spread from Britain in the north west and south east to the inland sea where Rome, the capital was situated. From there it extended further east west to another even larger sea, even though he could not imagine anything so large. They eventually crested a rise and saw a whole valley full of tents. The General and Rosanna had stopped so abruptly that Hugh almost walked into them. Priam was pointing out something to Rosanna and she, like Hugh, was truly amazed at this sight.

They looked at the vast array of tents, all pitched in line with soldiers hurrying in between, there were a number of small buildings that were obviously where General Priam and most of his senior staff were going to stay. After pointing out various things to Rosanna, the general continued to walk towards the small group of buildings. Rolex said to Hugh, "the general will take you to the married couples quarters, but I will expect you tomorrow at the valley, where I will have your standard weapons ready for you, together with the rest of your normal equipment that you will be expected to carry on campaign," He indicated himself and Crelux, "And so we will see you bright and early tomorrow morning." With that they left.

Hugh hurried at once to join General Priam and Rosanna just as they arrived by one of the small stone buildings. General Priam was saying to Rosanna, "This room will be yours until we receive the order to move. You are fortunate, as one of my other married couples has only just left, so make yourself comfortable as I expect that it will be at least twenty days before we receive orders to march." He then left them alone in their new surrounding.

"What did the general say to you my love?" Hugh asked.

"He asked how long we had been together, yet he presumed that we were already married, so I think that we must presume that we are, after all it is a very simple formality, do you not agree?" she enquired.

"Certainly my love, you are definitely all I want," he replied. They walked around in their own room which was divided into two smaller areas, one of them was obviously the bedroom and the other the main living and eating area, complete with a fire pit and a few cooking utensils.

"We have a short while before they supply dinner," she advised him.

"However, I think that we have time to test the bed," she said, with a twinkle in her eye and led him to the bed where she confessed, "I cannot get enough of you."

Early the next morning Hugh left Rosanna and walked towards his new cohort, the area that Centurion Rolex had indicated on the previous day. He was directed to the Centurion's mess tent, where he found Rolex in discussion with a couple of other Centurions and also Centurion Crelux. Hugh stood and cleared his throat noisily to let them know that he was there. "Ah Hugh," exclaimed Rolex. "I am glad that you found me, if you follow me I will take you over to the quartermaster's stores, where you will be issued all your equipment and your new uniform. Can your wife make any alterations if necessary?"

"Yes sir, she is very good with altering clothes, providing that she will have the time, only I do not know exactly how much time she will have, you see she has been asked to help out in the kitchens, so I do not know yet how much free time."

"Oh well, she will probably start with fairly light duties, so I am sure that she will have plenty of time," said Rolex. Hugh followed him to the quartermaster's stores, where he was surprised to see so much equipment and was even more amazed when he was given his new uniform, that he knew needed quite a lot of alterations, as it was very large and he wondered who it had previously belonged to. It had obviously belonged to somebody else before, as it was slightly frayed and had been roughly mended. The previous owner must have been a larger man and the mend was over a rent where he had been killed from behind. The shift had been washed, but not for a while, as there was some stains that were obviously made by blood. Hugh was staggered by the amount of the equipment that he had to carry, it was very heavy, even for him and Rolex told him that all the soldiers carried their personal equipment when they went on campaigns. Rolex told Hugh to carry his new equipment with him. This Hugh managed, although it was not easy and Hugh followed his new commander to where the cohort were training.

Hugh was relieved when Rolex told him to put down his equipment and was very pleased when Rolex showed him how to strap the rucksack and all the equipment on his person. He was surprised to realise that as well as the short sword he carried, he was also expected to carry two daggers, one of a conventional design, whilst the other was flat. As Hugh was staring at it, "Yes, that is for throwing," explained Rolex. Then in answer to Hugh's quizzical look, Rolex elaborated. "We only use the throwing dagger as a last resort, it is shaped that way so that it will go through the air and strike point first, we will show you how to throw it." As they watched, a short line of soldiers prepared to defend themselves against a larger group of soldiers who attacked the line in an undisciplined charge, very much like the form of fighting that Hugh's British tribe had used. Hugh was amazed to see how the short line of soldiers overlapped their shields and defended not themselves so much as their neighbour. This gave them more opportunity to swing and lunge their own weapons, which was very efficient but required complete faith in the men next to them. However, it was basically a far more effective way of fighting and Hugh realised that this was why the Romans had not yet been defeated.

They spent most of the day training and Hugh realised that it would take quite a while to acclimatise to this new form of warfare. He had no difficulty in using any of the weapons, although throwing the javelin would take quite a lot of practice, as it was far shorter than a normal spear and had to be thrown using a leather thong that was strapped around the wrist. He was relieved when the end of the day came and he lined up with the rest of the trainees for the evening meal where Rosanna was serving. Quite a few of his fellows remarked that she was very attractive. To this Hugh clearly pointed out that she was his wife and that he would kill anyone who attempted to shame her. One of the other trainee soldiers who Hugh liked and had befriended was called Gildar. He said, "You will have to watch Centurion Crelux, as I heard him commenting on what he would like to do with her, so keep a careful watch out for her!" Bearing this in mind he made his way back to his room, carrying his new uniform. He wondered whether or not he should mention what Gildar had said and thought that it would probably be right to alert her. He found that she was awaiting his return and was not surprised to hear what Gildar had told him.

After making him welcome with a very passionate embrace and making him comfortable, he told her all that Gildar had mentioned, but was surprised to learn that she already knew about Centurion Crelux. She said, "It is you who must be careful Hugh, as I have heard from some of the other girls that he uses the threat of flogging a trainee soldier, just so he can lift the charge of having the flogging providing that he has the women himself." Hugh was alarmed by this, but realised that it made sense, but wondered whether there was a way to overcome this danger.

Hugh slept well that night, although he did have a very strange dream about Rosanna being manhandled by Centurion Crelux. However when he woke up he never remembered it, although it must have been at the back of his mind, because whenever he threw the javelin, he imagined that the dummy he was aiming at was Centurion Crelux. Nonetheless this was effective, as it helped improve his javelin throwing. Even Centurion Rolex remarked on how Hugh's training was coming along. He said to Hugh, "I will hopefully be able to take you on our next campaign, I am expecting to hear about in the next ten days. I think we will be sailing north to Britain, where you came from. Have you any knowledge of the country?"

"Well yes," replied Hugh, "But only part of the south east, that was where I grew up. I would be very pleased to see Londinium, the new large town that you are building on the river that we call The Thames."

During the next few days Hugh continued his training and was watched by Centurion Crelux, who made very snide remarks about Hugh's use of the sword, although Hugh knew that he could easily out-fight anyone in single combat, because he had been a gladiator and the Roman short sword was his preferred weapon. He managed to ignore the remarks, even though they became more and more provocative. Eventually Centurion Rolex came over and asked why Centurion Crelux was being so rude about his trainee. Many of the other trainee soldiers were surprised to see the two centurions arguing, although Hugh knew that Centurion Crelux was trying to provoke him into retaliation so that he could put him on charge and then take him on one side and offer to have the charge lifted, if Hugh allowed him to have his wicked way with Rosanna. Eventually Centurion Crelux wondered off mumbling to himself.

The long awaited orders finally arrived and Hugh saw a horseman ride up to General Priam and deliver a scroll with the seal of Caesar stamped in beeswax, that covered all the possible ways opening the scroll. General Priam took the scroll and opened the beeswax with his dagger and read the orders and asked for all his centurions to come to him and disappeared into his own tent. There was a lot of speculation about what the orders contained and where the 9th Legion would be sent. There was a lot of discussion about whether they would return to Italy or go north west to where the Romans were fighting against the Huns on the north of their empire. However it became apparent that the information that Hugh had been given was perfectly correct and they were told that in the next twenty days they would be sailing north to Britain to go north from Londinium to fight against the invading tribes who were called the Picts and Scots. When Hugh told Rosanna that evening, she said, "I too have some news for you," and then almost taunting him by drawing out the moment, she finally relented and said, "I think I am going to have your baby." Hugh simply looked stunned, but then smiled and Rosanna smiled as well until Hugh actually threw back his head and punch the air saying, "Yes that's great!"

Hugh went to see General Priam and was allowed into his tent by the guards. General Priam looked up from his table that was littered with scraps of papyrus, where he had been working out the previsions needed for the legion. He looked up and asked, "what is it Hugh? You look quite excited!"

"Thank you for seeing me General, you are quite right I am excited. You see my wife has told me that she is expecting our first child."

The General's face lit up, "Congratulations my boy, I am very pleased for you. However it does mean that we will have to arrange suitable accommodation for Rosanna while you are on campaign."

He regarded Hugh thoughtfully before speaking again. "I think that the best thing that I can arrange is for Rosanna to go back to Rome and stay with my younger sister, who has her own young family. You see my orders are to march north from Londinium to quell the tribe and then return to Rome. I think that will suit Rosanna and hopefully you will come back from the campaign in one piece, so when you return with me to Rome you shall find your wife with your first child. We will have to work quickly as most of the soldiers with families are being sent home tomorrow, so bring Rosanna here after the evening meal and I will have written an introductory scroll to my sister and given the necessary permit for her to travel to Rome." He simply turned back to his work, indicating that the interview was over. Hugh returned to Rosanna and told her the good news, before he went back to his training.

Gradually the news of Rosanna leaving; spread throughout the legion. The only person who did not seem pleased was Centurion Crelux, who felt that he had been cheated. But still intending to steal Rosanna from Hugh, he thought that it was even better this way for if Hugh did not come back from the campaign, obviously engineered by himself there would be Rosanna in Rome with a baby and no father. Yes, it was definitely better this way because he could have her for himself. All it needed was careful preparation so that Hugh's death could not be traced to him, so with a sly smile he went to watch the final training session. He fell in behind centurion Rolex who was watching the final training of the new trainees. It was won by Hugh, who scored very well in all the tests, particularly sword fighting as he beat the trainee soldier without difficulty. "Young Hugh did very well Rolex, I think you should ensure that he marches in the first rank of your cohort, most of the British tribe will fly from us in terror, as they have never faced disciplined forces before. I think that this campaign should be easy!"

"I am relieved to hear you say that my friend, I thought that you did not like the lad."

"Oh no Rolex, it was obvious to me that he had the makings of a good soldier, he simply needed someone to encourage him and I thought that a little provocation was needed. You will now see that I was right," said Centurion Crelux. The two centurions walked back to their mess, discussing how they would arrange the accommodation for the legion on the twenty Roman galleys that would take the 9th Legion to cross the English Channel, and then sail or row up the River Thames to Londinium.

After beating all the other trainee soldiers in the final test, Hugh returned to meet Rosanna and give her the exciting news that she would be going to General Priam's sisters in Rome, while he went on campaign with the rest of the 9th Legion. He told her to pack her belongings, of which there were very few, so she was very quick and went with him to see the General. The guards outside the General's tent were expecting them, so issued them directly into the General's quarters. Priam was sitting just as he had been that morning, although everything was now sorted out neatly on the table in front of him. "Ah, there you are and the lovely Rosanna. I trust Hugh has told you that I am sending you to live with my sister in Rome."

"Yes General," said Rosanna quietly.

"There is nothing to be afraid of, my dear," said the General. "You will find my younger sister is very nice and lives in a splendid villa just north of Rome, in a town called Pisa." The General had obviously mistaken Rosanna's meekness for uncertainty and he wanted to reassure her that she would be welcome. "You see my sister has three sons, so she knows how to look after young children, in fact she will probably expect you to look after them when she goes out with her husband. He is a Senator." He caught a look in Hugh's eye and chuckled, "Do not worry Hugh, he is not Senator Latitch, although he knows the evil beast." Hugh was surprised to hear of the General refer to the Senator as an evil beast, yet this warmed him more towards his General. Hugh left Rosanna with the General, as she was to travel back to Rome with the ox cart that would be leaving on the long overland journey through Gaul to enter Italy in the northwest where there was a pass through the Alps. Hugh returned feeling strangely alone, even though he had only been living with Rosanna for less than eighty days, but started to think of the interesting sea voyage that he would be making and of the fascinating sight of Londinium.

They marched to the coast the next morning and Hugh was quite surprised that he was with the very best in his cohort. They were all veteran soldiers, tried and tested, although they welcomed Hugh into their company. He soon realised that they had all heard of his ability with weapons and many of them knew of his fight with Adobe. They boarded the Roman galley and went to the large cabins below the deck, but above where the slaves were sitting, chained to the rowing bench and where the drummer sat to hammer out the rowing rhythm. Hugh thought that he was lucky not to be one of the slaves, as they only averaged three years life on the rowing benches, before they dropped dead from exhaustion. Their lacerated bodies were then thrown to the sharks. Hugh came to know his fellow soldiers and although many of them were introduced to Hugh, his favourites were two soldiers who were called Timothy and Marcus. They both came from an island in the Mediterranean Sea, that they called Rodos. They told Hugh that it was only a small island to the east of Italy, but to the west of a large island called Cyprus. Hugh sat between his two new friends and later unrolled his sleeping mat between them. He told them that he had come from Britain, so he was then asked all about the country, but could not tell them very much as he only knew the south east corner of Britain where he had lived before becoming a gladiator.

*   *   *   *   *

Rosanna sat in the ox cart with some of the other wives and looked back at the soldiers camp wishing that she was still with Hugh, even though she knew that she was now safe from Centurion Crelux. The ox wagons were very slow and although she was quite comfortable, she felt that she would rather be walking. She suddenly realised that the girl sitting next to her was speaking, so she turned and said, "I am sorry Lydia, what did you just ask me?"

"I thought you were not listening as you had a far away gleam in your eye. You must not worry about Hugh, I am sure that he will be alright, the Romans have the finest army in the world, they have never been beaten, so I am sure Hugh will come back to you in Pisa."

"Thank you, Lydia, for those kind words and I apologise for not listening earlier, it is just that Hugh and I were only together for such a short time!" The ox cart trundled along on the straight Roman road and the soldiers' camp was lost behind them as they saw the lights before them. The wagon driver called back over his soldier, "We are just coming to where we will be staying tonight, there is a nice place by the lake where you ladies can sleep. I will stop the wagon by the lake, where the oxen will be quite happy."

Rosanna sat beside Lydia discussing her idea of walking so they spoke to the ox driver the next day and asked whether they could walk beside the ox cart. The driver replied, "Most certainly, but do not go beyond the soldiers marching in front or fall behind the soldiers in the rear. You see, although this is part of the Roman Empire, there are still some unruly tribes around, so that is why we have to travel with an escort." So they walked beside the ox cart and when one of the women queried why Rosanna preferred to walk, she replied saying, "Pregnancy is not an illness and while I am still able to walk without difficulty because the baby does not show yet, I prefer to walk." By this time they had made friends with the wagon driver who complained that they were now on one of the roads that the old Franks had built along side the large river from which was a tributary from the small lake where they had stopped on the previous day. The driver told them that this route followed the river all the way to the largest town called Paris, where there was a bridge over the river. True to their promise, the girls kept near to the ox wagon, but they took four complete days before they reached Paris where the road crossed the river on a bridge made from stone that had at least twenty arches to it. Neither of the girls had seen a large bridge and asked the ox driver about whether he knew who had built it, when he answered and said, "This bridge was build by the Romans, you can always tell because the bridge is made of arches, you see the Romans realised that an arch was stronger than just ordinary supports, unlike the Greeks who's empire was almost as large as ours, but they did not use arches, so it is no great wonder that we took over their empire."

Once over the bridge the Roman road continued in a fairly straight line and this made the wagon driver a lot happier and they made faster progress although it was still almost twenty days before they saw a distant mountain ahead of them. When Lydia asked the ox driver about the mountain he told her that it was called The White Mountain or Mount Blanc by which name it is still called today.

"Why is it called Mount Blanc?" asked Lydia

"Because it is always covered in snow, well certainly the top of the mountain," replied the wagon driver. After a slight pause he continued to speak, "You two girls seem to always be asking me a lot of questions! However I enjoy talking to you so please continue to ask me questions, I am more than happy to talk to you lovely ladies." Both Rosanna and Lydia were very pleased by this comment as they wished to learn many things, but did not wish to be a nuisance. "Why does the snow never melt on the top of the mountain?" asked Rosanna. "We have mountains in Gaul but the snow melts in the summer and Hugh, my husband was telling me that they have mountains in Britain but again the snow on the mountains does not stay in summer," she commented.

"Well the mountains in Italy are just the same, but if we go northeast the mountains there have snow all the year round. May I ask you to call me Arte as all my friends do?"

"Yes Arte, now you can call me Rosanna and my friend is Lydia, it is so nice to be friends."

They continued southeasterly for the next few days and then it was very misty in the early morning. Arte told them that the lake that they were coming to caused the mist and, sure enough, when they crested the next rise they saw many large lakes and the mountain ahead of them. "We will have to go over the pass by the mountain, but it will be fairly chilly, so I suggest that you both wear your cloaks even though it is still late summer and quite warm down here. The road goes gradually up higher and higher and then we come to the pass around the mountain. Now there, there is a river of ice and we have to cross. I believe that when you go higher it becomes colder, even though you are nearer to the sun," he chuckled. He proved to be correct and it was quite chilly, particularly if there was any wind. "I think there is a storm coming," said Arte, "as my right ankle always aches when there is a storm coming. It has been like that ever since I broke it as a youngster when I was in the army, that is why I am just a wagon driver now, it ruined my career and I always walk with a limp," he groaned dramatically, to emphasise the point. They came to a small village where they rested for the night. The wagon was put into a barn and Rosanna and Lydia slept in a real bed, which made a wonderful change from sleeping beneath the stars on the hard earth.

They had reached the river of ice and Arte put a light chain around the wagon's wheels and leather bags over the oxen's hooves with small iron spikes, that would help the oxen keep their footing and the chain around the wheel would stop it from slipping on the river of ice. They crossed quite easily, without any problems. "You see the river of ice moves so very slowly that you cannot see it," he explained. Once they were across he stopped and they helped him to remove the chains and the bags from around the wheels and hooves. "Thank you very much girls," said Arte, "we are almost in Italy now, the road starts to go down and it will become warmer."

"That's good," said Lydia, "I won't miss it, I hated all the thunderstorms we had the other night even though we were undercover, I always become frightened when there is a thunderstorm."

"I know what you mean," agreed Rosanna, "I too am frightened. My parents used to tell us that it is the gods rolling around in their sleep, what do you think Arte?"

"Well, it is certainly something to do with the gods, I believe that they say that Mars is the God of War and Mars can be seen in the sky at night, so I think there must be something in that. You see Mars often is said to bring battles, but nobody really knows or is sure about what the gods want. I mean the soldiers call him Mithras and so pray to Mithras. There is a very secret ceremony, whenever you are in the army you can become a Mithras soldier, but it is a very special ceremony and to be a Mithras soldier means that you have fought very well and broken many shield walls."

"Yes, it is what my husband told me, he says that he wants to become a Mithraic."

"Well he may reach that goal, if what you have told me about him is true Rosanna. Being a gladiator must mean that he was very good at fighting, so I am sorry for the people that he fights against, and I am sure he is very good."

Arte was perfectly correct, it did become quite a bit warmer as they descended and very soon they passed a sign that told them they were in Italy and Arte really cheered up. "We are now safe from any brigands or bandits, because we are now in a civilised country where nobody is silly enough to misbehave while Caesar rules," he claimed emphatically. "I know you want to go to Pisa, Rosanna, but do you have any plans, Lydia? I have been told to take all the rest of the ladies to the main barrack in Rome."

"Well we were talking about that last night, I was wondering if we could stay together, as we used to work together, but I don't know whether General Priam's sister will want another maid," she look enquiringly at Arte.

"Well I will have a talk with her, I know the lady quite well and it is the least I can do for you. I do not remember enjoying a journey as much as this one. I am going to ask that we are allowed to have companions to travel with, it only makes the journey far more enjoyable," he said with a roguish wink. It was another three days before they came to Pisa, where Arte was true to his word. Arte stopped and spoke to General Priam's sister, who was very pleased to take Lydia as a servant as well, because she always needed staff and they were soon to find out why.

* * * * *

The sea is very treacherous as it was very cold when they boarded the galley and rowed into the British channel. But very soon the waves became very large and the galley was rolling and pitching, which made a lot of the soldiers seasick, although Hugh was quite used to the sea and its fickle nature, that doesn't seem to depend upon the weather overhead. Many of the soldiers from the Mediterranean area had never seen such large waves and it made them realise why

31

Britain was only recently added to the Roman Empire, even though you could see some of the coast of Britain from Gaul. Before the galley swung in a north westerly direction and finally rounded the Isle of Tenet and began to row into the calmer waters of what became the River Thames estuary. The sea voyage had lasted for five days before they saw the northern bank of the estuary and Timothy said to Hugh, "By the gods I am glad that we are now in calmer water, for I don't think that there is anything left in my stomach, I have thrown it all over the side and I am not the only one. In fact it is only you that I believe has enjoyed the voyage." He was perfectly correct, for apart from Hugh and a few of the slaves, most of the men were in very poor shape and lying around groaning in puddles of their own vomit. Eventually General Priam came out of his cabin on to the deck, looking no better than most of his men. However, he noticed where they were and gave instructions that all the galleys should be washed down with sea water, to make them more respectable as they would soon reach Londinium.

The galley looked very smart as it rowed up the river with the tide and docked on the northern bank with the other galley following in its wake. The men were most please to have their feet back on solid earth and, remarkably quickly, seemed to recover their fitness, because they were fit, fighting men and were soon cheerful as they all fell in to their cohorts, and once again the 9th Legion marched proudly in to the streets of the new city. Hugh was amazed at the size of the city and he had been told by none other than General Priam that it was almost two thousand passes along each of its four walls, which formed a square. They entered the barracks and were all allocated their temporary sleeping quarters. These were special huts and had been erected very quickly and smelt of new wood that had been cut to make the furniture. Hugh knew that most of the wood that had been used was called pine. It grew very quickly compared to the darker oak and beech that was used to make the more solid furniture in the officers quarters, that seemed rather splendid and looked out of place for what was meant to be temporary. The barrack huts that they had been allocated had a row of three bunk beds and Hugh was given the top bunk, while Timothy and Marcus were on the bunks below him.

Centurion Rolex issued orders that they should take full rest and then line up outside were they would be inspected, and each man would have his weapons checked to ensure that the sea air had not created any rust on the weapons. These orders were barked out so that all the men knew that any weapon that showed any sign of rust would mean that its owner would be in trouble, so they all checked their weapons very carefully. Because he had been used to the sea air, Hugh had covered all his weapons with mutton fat and when he explained why he was doing this to Timothy and Marcus they had joined in using this trick to ensure that their weapons stayed clean and free from rust.

When they lined up for the inspection, Hugh noticed that Centurion Crelux inspected his own cohort very quickly and joined Centurion Rolex to help him inspect his cohort's weapons. Almost predictably he made straight for the platoon that Hugh was in and began looking at the weapons that each soldier had placed in front of him. He picked up one of Hugh's daggers and with a very quick slight of hand changed it for a rusty dagger. He called to his fellow centurion and said, "Have you seen this appalling specimen?" All the time glaring maliciously at Hugh.

"Is this your dagger, Hugh?" enquired Rolex.

"No Sir, certainly not. All my weapons have my initials carved in the handle." He was about to add that Centurion Crelux had swapped it, when he checked himself and noticed that Marcus had shaken his hand behind the centurion, as he mouthed the words, "Don't push your luck."

"You can see that dagger does not have my initials carved in the handle." At that precise moment there were three sharp whistle blasts summoning all the centurions to General Priam. As the centurions left, putting all the weapons that they were inspecting into a pile, Hugh breathed a sigh of relief and thanked Marcus for mouthing his warning.

"No problem, Hugh. Centurion Crelux can turn very nasty at times, so I thought it best to warn you." There was quite a lot of talking in the ranks while the centurions were receiving orders. This was quite normal as many of the soldiers took the opportunity to relax and not remain at attention. The centurions came and the chatter ceased, as the soldiers reformed into ordinary ranks.

Centurion Rolex cleared his throat before saying, "You are all to take up your weapons and return to your barrack huts, before we leave for the next town to the north, which is called Colchester. We will be staying there for a few days before we go north again. We will be aiming for York, but the tribes in the hills north of Colchester can be very treacherous, so we will be alright until we reach Colchester, and that will take less than two days full march." They gratefully fell out and returned to their barrack huts, collecting the discarded weapons on their way.

They were up early the next morning, to commence their march to Colchester. Few realised that this would be their last look at Londinium, but marched away with a jaunty air to their stride, singing one of the legion's marching songs. The Roman road had recently been finished and they made excellent time on their march, with a brief overnight halt, when many of the soldiers slept on the ground, not even bothering about making a bivouac or even pitching a tent, as it was late summer and quite warm. They marched in to the new Colchester around mid-morning, having started marching early, which was just as well as they had to help build their new barracks. Hugh remembered much of his former life in Britain, when he used to live by hunting for the cooking pot. He was in much demand and his cohort were soon noticeably more advanced than anyone else. This was realised by General Priam, who complimented Centurion Rolex on his cohorts ability, much to the annoyance of Centurion Crelux. When the centurions were in council with the General that evening, the general said, "Your cohort is putting all the rest to shame Rolex, can you explain why?"

"Yes Sir, it is because one of my soldiers comes from Britain, it is the lad who was a gladiator, he has remembered most of his old woodcraft. You see most of the men come from the Mediterranean area and are unused to foraging in this country, but Hugh knows where the animals can be found and what use they can be put to, I think that I would like to promote him, with your permission of course."

"Yes, I am glad that he has proved useful, make a note that he should be in line for the next Sergeant's post that becomes available." Much to Centurion Crelux's annoyance, Hugh gained even greater prestige on the very next day. When Hugh returned to camp he unwittingly rescued Centurion Crelux from being trampled by a runaway stag. It was not until Hugh realised that he had shot the beast that he realised his mistake, "I should never have shot the beast, but let it finish off Crelux for me," he said, much to everybody's amusement. On the last evening in Colchester General Priam asked for Hugh to be summoned to him and he asked, "Everybody speaks highly of you Hugh, although all along I thought you only knew the southeast of Britain?"

"That's perfectly true Sir, yet all of Britain is quite similar, so until we go much further north and we come to what we refer to as mountains. Although I believe that you would only call them hills because they are not very high, although there were many strange and frightening tales told to us about them, but that was many years ago when I was only in my teens, so I was only a boy really and, well you know how tales do frighten the youngster, it's all part of growing up I suppose!"

General Priam laughed. "Yes my young man, I know exactly what you mean, I think I will move you from your cohort to be with my own staff, for you would be of more use to me than where you are at present."

"Thank you General, sorry but I would like to be with my two companions, they are both from Rodos in the Mediterranean, yet they are very keen to learn about Britain and I also am learning about life in the Mediterranean. I believe that their island is not dissimilar from where you come from. Would it be possible for them to come with me?"

"Alright you young rascal, I am becoming used to your requests. Go and tell them to bring their belongings and you can all join me. I have three of my own men who can join Centurion Rolex to make his numbers up." Hugh returned to tell Timothy and Marcus of their move, which they were all very pleased about.

When they finally marched north from Colchester, the new Roman road, which would lead them to York was unfinished, although its route was clearly marked and Hugh marvelled at the construction. In many places the ground was excavated by up to four cubits and this would later be filled with pebbles and coarse sand before paving slabs of dressed stone would be laid neatly on a slightly convex cross section which allowed any rain to run off the road, and it would run in special channels that would occasionally run into purpose made soakaways. Where possible the materials that were used were taken from local quarries, dug on route and it was most noticeable that when they were about four days from Colchester the Romans had found large areas in the flat lands, where there was clay which was suitably fine, and was dug out by the cart load and to be used to make pots or dishes for eating. Marcus and Timothy told Hugh that this was used by the top Romans, in preference to the iron or tin plates and cooking vessels used by the army, which were both heavy and required a lot of cleaning, particularly when they cooked on open wood fires, although Hugh knew the best type of wood for cooking, it varied according to what was being cooked. They would use the pinewood when they required something that burns brightly and fiercely, or the denser hard woods like oak or beech if they were stewing meat. The only one who was displeased by Hugh's move was Centurion Crelux, as this took him well away from the main legion, although Crelux knew that in the time of battle the main job that Hugh would be used for would be to guard the legion's eagle standard around which the strongest and best defenders would rally. There had only been one eagle lost to date and that had been lost fighting the Huns in the lands north of Gaul. Crelux was not sure which legion had been defeated, but he thought it was the 38th. But the 9th Legion had a fine reputation and was commanded by an excellent General.

Travelling on what was more like a track, rather than on a straight road, the distance they covered was much less than normal. They passed through lands that had not even been cleared of basic vegetation. Therefore, it was advisable for small parties of soldiers to be sent ahead and on each side of the main legion, often making plenty of noise to deter any potential brigands or outlaws from the path of the main body of men, not that they feared such individuals, but General Priam thought it better to subjugate the local tribe into peaceful co-existence with their new masters. When they came to any British village, the General was very strict about the behaviour of his men and he would not let them destroy any of the sheep or cattle belonging to the British tribes, but would prefer to buy any of the meat or grain that had been grown or cultivated, ensuring that reasonable payment was given and also that the men were well behaved towards the natives. Hugh realised that this form of behaviour would endear the Roman way of life. They were also making it far easier for the road builders who would be following the men, making the road that would eventually make it far easier to travel between the large towns.

Eventually, after moving more west than directly north, they crossed a large area where the sea would often flood the land and Hugh found that by climbing one of the tallest trees he could spy out the land ahead. He could see a fairly large hill to the north, where there was a settlement. This was reported to General Priam, who decided that the legion would march there and establish it as a base. Thus the town of Lincoln was established as a Roman garrison. After a storm, it was decided to stay for five days to fully explore the surrounding countryside, to reprovision the legions stores of meat because the land had appeared to be less hospitable, and it was a fairly large river ahead. It was here that Hugh was promoted to become a Sergeant, when a vacancy occurred, because of a foraging party that was being led by a Sergeant who was not very sensible and who challenged one of the native chiefs to a man to man fight. He did not realise that the locals were totally unused to such behaviour and also did not fight fairly, as they considered such a form of combat was quite silly, so that was how the first casualty occurred.

Hugh was far more sensible and made friends with the tribal chief, as he knew the language, although understanding the local dialect was not easy, he managed to communicate and arrange to have a lot of the meat and grain that was cultivated and herded by the locals. He also told General Priam that the local chief had invited them to take part in a wild boar hunt, which would add more meat to the legion, so obviously the General was very much in favour of the idea. Hugh selected ten men whom he commanded; they included Marcus and Timothy, his close friends. They left the rest of the legion and went with the tribe chief who took ten of his men with him. They also had some of the tribe's hounds to help flush their quarry out to the waiting spears. When they moved towards a thicket Hugh realised that he had become slightly separated from his men although the tribe's chieftain was near at hand. There was a boar in the thicket and the boar suddenly charged at him, only just allowing him time to level the spear, which he planted into the hind flank just above the right leg and directly towards the beast's heart. Fortunately tusks flashed a fingers width from Hugh's face just before Hugh's spear hit home and the beast was impaled, dying on top of Hugh, who was soaked in blood and urine as the dying beast emptied its bladder. By the time that Hugh was free from the carcass of the boar and was helped up to his feet by the tribe's chief, it was quite dark and rather than trying to find their way back to the legion, they thought it would be advisable to remain in the forest, where they found a hollow tree and made a camp. The hollow tree was shared by the chief of the tribe and by Hugh, as they had now become good friends, with the rest of the men making bivouacs in the forest around them. They had plenty to eat, as meat from the boar, although tasting rather tough, went well with the berries that the English picked from the surrounding bushes.

Meanwhile back at the legions camp, the disappearance of Hugh was being discussed by the centurions. Despite Centurion Rolex thinking that Hugh had taken shelter for the night and would return the next day, Centurion Crelux was insisting that he had made friends with the local chief and would not return to the legion and voiced feelings to General Priam, who sided with Centurion Rolex. He said, "Hugh would not do that, particularly as he has a wife who is expecting their first child! She is by now hopefully with my sister back in Italy, where Rosanna will have the child. You see my sister runs a school for children where many of the soldier's wives go, for their children to be taught and brought up in proper Roman fashion and therefore your ideas are ridiculous Crelux. I am sure that Hugh will be back with us tomorrow." Most of the Centurions agreed with

General Priam and also thought that Centurion Crelux was trying to make trouble. Many of them knew that he wanted to have Hugh out of the way when he would be able to have his chance with Rosanna. He could offer her far more with Hugh out of the way. Even Centurion Rolex knew of Centurion Crelux's way, even though he was a friend, he had seen the way that Crelux had gained his rank by devious plotting, as well as being at the right place at the right time.

On the following day Hugh came back to the legion with plenty of meat from not only the boar that he slew, but also from the many wild pigs that had been killed and their sow. This greatly pleased the entire legion and everybody benefited from this. The only person who was not pleased by Hugh's return was Centurion Crelux. It was by now common knowledge that Crelux disliked Hugh and many people knew why this was and this made Crelux even more bitter towards Hugh, if that were possible. Hugh went to see General Priam, when he told the General that to the northwest there were some mountains, where many of the local tribes said there was some very hard stone. General Priam said, "We had some men who have come with us to explore the rocks and possibly find iron in the hills, which you call mountains," he chuckled.

"Yes General, I know that one of the things that the legion needs to do is to find out what mineral deposits are available in the land, I believe that the Romans have already found tin and copper deposits in the southwest corner of Britain."

"You are quite right, we have found tin and copper, which is needed to make bronze," explained General Priam tapping his breastplate as he exclaimed to emphasise the point.

They left that area and moved north once more aiming for York. They gradually moved into a valley and sighted a river, not as large as the Thames, but large enough to pass as a considerable barrier. This they only managed to cross by having to make a raft as it was too deep to ford easily. Although Hugh could, and managed to secure a stout rope on the opposite bank, by tying a lighter rope around his waist and swimming across the river at a fairly calm stretch, having firstly taken off all his body armour, like his breastplate and grieves, which covered the front of his legs from the ankle to knee. Hugh secured the rope to a large tree and then pulled a thicker rope across the river that he also had to secure. He was fascinated by the ropes and by the way that they were often secured at their ends by being dipped in tar or vegetable oil or even whipped with a very thin cord, that was made from the contents of small animals, or so he was told. His old life as a fisherman, before he was captured by General Priam, made him very interested in ropes. In particular about the way that this rope was tightened by using a double sheave pulley block, that was attached to a single sheave pulley block, which when pulled made a three-to-one advantage in strength of the direction that it was being pulled. Therefore when the men pulled this rope, it became as taught as an iron bar. Hugh asked Marcus about this and was told that it was believed to be used in his own country of Rodos when the Greeks had built an enormous bronze plated structure of a warrior that collapsed over three hundred years previously, but he went on to tell Hugh that he believed that the builders had probably taken the idea from the Persians when they had built a huge structure which was still standing and believed to be one of the Wonders Of The World. He also told Hugh about a river he had seen on the southern shore of the Mediterranean Sea, which was probably ten days by galley from his own island. Hugh was also very interested in how the ropes were spliced, either back on themselves or to form a loop, called an eye. The chief of the British tribe, who had befriended Hugh, told him that he would not cross the river as his tribes boundary was the river and terrible things would happen to them if they crossed into another tribes area, so Hugh had to reluctantly say goodbye to him.

They travelled north towards York and the hills to their left became more rugged and while they were looking, even General Priam remarked about this when he asked Hugh why the tribe's chief had not followed them. Hugh said, "This land belongs to a different tribe, I believe that they are called the Iceni and they are led by a Queen, who is called Boadicea. She is held in great fear by all subjects, who apparently wear very little in the way of clothing. They often paint themselves blue with a dye that they call woad, which makes them very frightening."

"Yes, that I can well imagine, let's hope we do not run into them," said the General, thoughtfully.

Hugh left him as he was calling all his centurions to him, as well as the other senior officers in the legion. Hugh wandered back to his own bed and mentioned about the Iceni people and what he had told General Priam.

"I am not surprised that the General was worried about us running into them, because they do sound very frightening," said Marcus.

"I am afraid that that is not all, but I did not want to alarm the General any more than I did, but I believe they also twist their hair into spikes with cow dung. As you can imagine, that makes them even more frightening!"

"By the gods, yes, it certainly does, it scares the shit out of me," commented Marcus.

The further north they went their pace became slower and slower each day with slightly more difficult country to cross, even though there were no major obstacles, all the rivers were fordable and even the hills were not too steep. There was an absence of any normal creature like deer or fox, and at certain times of the day when it would be normal to hear bird song there was an evil, pressing quietness that pervaded the very air and gave everybody the feeling that they were being watched. It was very weird and creepy; nobody was keen to even go on patrol and very occasionally when a small foraging party came back without managing to kill any animals, the legion had to rely on the food that they had brought with them. After at least five more days when they were beginning to start rationing their food, some of the men who went on foraging parties came back with reports that they had seen some of the frightening Britons that Hugh had described to General Priam. Most of these stories were disregarded, being attributed to frightened soldiers, who thought that when the mist that often covered the ground suggested strange and freighting shapes. This simply added to everybody's worries and even the elite fighting men like Hugh began to start worrying. General Priam called Hugh to his tent one morning, together with some of his other trusted lookouts who knew the land and he confided his fears with them, so he decided to send a whole cohort in the direction of York. The following morning a complete cohort, comprising of about one hundred and twenty men with five centurions, set out and they marched away trying to be cheerful even singing one of their marching songs, which were about the 9th Legion and they sang of its many conquests. That night there was a thunderstorm, where the sky was suddenly illuminated by vast stabs of lightning. The dark sky overhead reverberated with the deep rumbling of the thunder, that crashed around the hilltops and sent echoes into every ear, even those wrapped in blankets or shirts. The storm continued into the next day and the early evening, when it finally broke with cascades of cold rain that soaked everybody. By the following morning nothing was seen of the cohort, although they had strict instructions to send back frequent reports. They were never seen again.

By now everybody was concerned for their own safety and there were many who predicted that they should go no further north, but return to the friendlier tribal Britons. However, General Priam, who correctly said, "The garrison at York is expecting us and by my reckoning we should sight the battlements in a day or two", quashed this. So it was decided to press forward and sure enough the next day the garrison was sighted and the greatly relieved legion marched into York, only to find that the garrison was in a worse condition than the 9th Legion. When General Priam met the garrison governor, the governor told him that they had been unable to receive the local tribute from the surrounding tribes, who were all in alliance with this new queen, who called herself Boadicea. They had been unable to keep any animals outside the garrison, or harvest any produce, so they were all on short rations and he hoped that the 9th Legion would be able to bring them some food. "I am sorry, but my men are very much in the same condition that yours are in. We were hoping that you would be able to provide us with the necessary food. In fact, we have already lost one cohort to this savage queen," and he went on to relate the tale of how the cohort had disappeared during the thunderstorm. "No trace has been seen of them since the thunderstorm. All the parties that I sent out scouting came back with the same news that there is nothing to be seen and no game to replenish our food stores."

"Right you are General, I am very pleased that I now have a commander of a legion who outranks me, so you are obviously in charge." He paused, and looked down at his sandled feet and shuffled awkwardly, before looking up and speaking again. "Well General, what do you propose we do?"

"There is obviously no point in sitting here, starving to death, so I will take the whole legion, plus any troops that you have who are willing to fight the Iceni queen. We will show her how Rome treats its enemies."

* * * * *

General Priam's sister was similar to the General in looks with the same strong jaw line and similar eyes beneath heavy bushy eyebrows, which had obviously been plucked to make her more attractive. She even had the same sandy coloured hair that was starting to go grey. Yet she was quite attractive and obviously very much in charge of everything that happened in this villa. Rosanna was quite surprised to see that she was surrounded by plenty of young children, who were charging around and chirping like sparrows, which she completely ignored, unless one of them stopped and asked her a direct question. Although the children were quite well behaved and they did not interrupt her as she asked the girls what they did. Rosanna said, "We worked together in the kitchens serving food for the soldiers, but we are not limited to working in the kitchens, in fact I like children and I used to teach them how to serve and make clothes. Now Lydia used to teach different languages, so you may like to use her as she also likes working with children."

"Thank you, Rosanna, I am sure that I can find suitable jobs for both of you. By the way, my name is Cynthia, but most of the children call me Miss Priam, as I run the villa as a home for soldiers' wives and their children, obviously until some of the children become older and join their fathers or seek work else where." She then took the girls through the villa to where there were some spare rooms where there was a separate entrance to the grounds. She asked the girls, "Presumably you do not mind sharing a room, but obviously I have noticed that you are pregnant, Rosanna, when is the baby due?"

"Not for at least one hundred days, but as I had to keep reminding Arte, pregnancy is not an illness and there is nothing really wrong with me, so I should not be excluded from any work, except lifting things."

"Yes, you are quite right and you will not receive any preferential treatment from me, until you go into labour, but obviously there are plenty of people to give you a hand with lifting anything, so you two girls bring your things in here then come and see me, but take your time to settle into your new room. Yes, it is your home now, so treat it as such." Then she left the girls to settle in. Their new room was very spacious and had a doorway that opened onto the orchard, where there were olive trees and some fruit trees that neither of the girls had seen before. They were unlike the fruit trees in Gaul, where there were many apples, but these fruits were bright yellow and bright orange, yet they had a very pleasant smell, although when they were inspected they were covered with a thick rind that was not edible, unlike the skin of an apple.

Rosanna and Lydia returned to their room and chose who would have each bed, before unpacking their belongings. This did not take very long as neither of the girls had brought many clothes with them. Once everything was sorted out they went in search of Cynthia to see about the work that she was arranging for them. They found her in the main villa's central room that were being used as a classroom for many of the older children. She clapped her hands and the room fell immediately into a silence as she introduced Rosanna and Lydia to the girls and told them that Rosanna would be teaching them her dressmaking skills, while Lydia would be teaching her language skills, which were basically the language of the Gauls and that of the Huns. She then asked the girls if they both wrote, to which they both answered in the affirmative, although Rosanna added, "We do write but not very well and probably could do with some practice."

"That is easily arranged, I myself am a teacher of reading and writing, but obviously we prefer to use Latin or possibly Greek, due to the Roman Empire having succeeded to the Greek Empire, but of course the Greeks did not have such a large empire as Caesar does, although the Greek Empire used to stretch further to the east, where there are dark skinned natives, just like those in the countries to the south of the Mediterranean Sea where we have not finished exploring beyond the large sandy deserts." Both girls started their teaching jobs the next day, they both enjoyed working for Cynthia and Rosanna found that she only really missed Hugh when she was not busy, but on the odd occasion when she quietly relaxing she often thought about what he would be doing. These thoughts often worried her, particularly as they had heard no news from Britain. When they had been in the villa for at least two months, after they had tasted the new fruits that they had seen, they experienced a shock when, without prior warning, a Roman Senator visited the villa, accompanied, as he always was, by his two large powerfully built but simple bodyguards. Rosanna immediately recognised Senator Latitch, who strutted around as if he owned the place. It was quite clear that even Cynthia detested the skinny, weak chinned, pot bellied, yet arrogant little man. He noticed Rosanna and came over, saying something to his bodyguards, who guffawed stupidly.

"I believe that I have seen you before. Are you not the wife off the gladiator, who was beaten, when I visited Aurolius? I wanted him killed, it was only General Priam who saved his life but I think that the Britons have done the job for me, as there has been an uprising in Britain. So it looks like General Priam is finished, but do not worry my dear as I am sure that I can find something for you to do, like keep my bed warm," he said.

* * * * *

The 9th Legion marched north from York, accompanied by reinforcements from the garrison, but these men were only volunteers, who simply had decided that they would rather die fighting than starve to death, so an impending doom permeated even the toughest man. The weather was now very chilly and they seemed to be drawn into wilder and rougher country where there were only rough ground with

45

only small stunted trees, that were now entirely leafless, as it was nearing the winter solstice. They had just forded one of the small rivers and came down from the hills to the east. The very air seemed damp and chilly, even General Priam was beginning to feel threatened and had just called his trumpeter to signal a rest, when the air was filled with heavy pounding and they looked to the ridge directly in front of them, where there was a fairly flat stretch of ground. The drumming was made by a vast horn of Iceni warriors, who were beating hollow logs with their stone war clubs. They were all big powerful men and were only clad in trews, with their arms and chest bare, despite the cold. They were covered in a blue dye, with their dark hair twisted into spikes, which made them very frightening. Yet they were nothing in comparison to their leader who was standing on a chariot. She was auburn haired, but had intricate whirls of the blue dye on her bare arms and shoulders, the power seemed to radiate from her and she held her sword aloft. The drumming ceased as abruptly as it had started and she pointed the sword directly at General Priam, who was sitting on his horse, but seemed diminished in her presence. She only said one word and in the British tongue, yet everybody realised what it meant. 'KILL'. And the might of the Iceni fell on the 9th Legion, whom they outnumbered by at least ten to one.

Queen Boadicea led the charge with the small yet sturdy, shaggy horses, leading the charge as the Legion rapidly rallied to their prearranged fighting formation. Hugh was in the central formation, guarding both the Legion's Eagle and also their General. The very sight of the auburn hair of the Queen racing down towards them in her speeding chariot, which had cruel knives projecting from the solid wheels, was a terrifying sight. Her horses had heavy leather breastplates and had heavy iron footplates that were strapped to their hooves, which could be heard even above the battle cries of the wild Iceni warriors. The Queen's chariot seemed to cut through the ranks, as if they were wheat before the Harvesters scythe. Hugh realised that there was little point in trying to save the beloved eagle and immediately thought of trying to protect General Priam, whom he saw being thrown from his white stallion, which was pierced by many javelins and arrows that were fired by the advancing Iceni. Having launched his own javelin he dived under the flying hooves of Boadicea's chariot to shield the General's body with his own, he was mainly but not completely successful, as although by some lucky chance, he was unhurt himself, General Priam's left leg was caught by one of the hooves and he could hear the bone break. The General must have fainted, either with pain or shock or even terror, yet Hugh knew that the general was no stranger to being in fear and would not flinch by the threat from the evil Queen, so surmised that it must have been from the pain in his leg, as he went slack although he was still breathing, albeit very shallowly. Hugh lay very still, as the sound of battle gradually died away, but he could hear voices near at hand spoken in a bastardised British tongue. He lay quite still half covering the General and realised that the 9th Legion was finished, although he could just about make out words and wondered if he should dare to open his eyes and stop pretending to feign being dead. That was a difficult decision, if he did not fear death himself, but wondered if there was a chance of rescuing the general and escaping. Here his thoughts returned to Rosanna and the baby, he thought that he would risk just a quick look, particularly as he could make out what was being said, even though it was in a very harsh British tongue and one the commanding voices was female and probably belonged to Queen Boadicea.

Hugh opened his eyes and quickly looked around, he saw that Queen Boadicea must have driven over the General, as there were marks on his legs where the chariot must have crossed, just above his knee where the bone was broken. Queen Boadicea must have returned as her chariot was only about fifteen passes away and she was giving orders to her tribal chiefs. Hugh closed his eyes and lay still again, trying to catch every word that was being said. "We must go forward to capture York and then we'll drive for the south, to free Britain from these domineering Romans. We can leave the women to ensure that all the dead are burnt and all the bones ground into dust as if they had never existed." After a while, during which more orders were given, Queen Boadicea eventually moved away, as Hugh could hear her chariot's wheels going forward and eventually they passed through the small river that they had previously crossed. Darkness was beginning to fall, just when he heard the harsh cackles of women who were butchering the dead corpses and taking any weapons or any valuables. He realised that he would have to try and drag the General's body and try to float it down river to escape, even though he didn't know the area at all, he knew that Britain was an island; so all rivers must lead to the sea. Hugh had previously been a fisherman before he was captured, and knew that rivers always contained fish, that would at least keep them alive. He saw that the women were gradually coming closer, although they had now lit many torches and were beginning to burn the dead. He therefore sat up and painfully rose to his feet, aching in every muscle and began to drag the General's body towards the small river. He was fortunate as none of the women noticed him, as they were blinded by the light of the fires and their torches and engrossed in their work of plundering the dead. He finally reached the sandy riverbank. He then took off the General's breastplate, shin grieves and wrist guards knowing that he'd have to try to keep the General's face above the water, therefore he kept only his dagger with him, as he lowered himself into the cold water. It was bloody cold and he thought that if he and General survived they would be very fortunate. Somehow he managed to keep the General afloat and kept going although it was completely dark and they were away from the battlegrounds and the river was joined by another stream and became even larger. Here it entered a wood, which sheltered them from any possible view, so Hugh dragged the General's body out and began to realise that he was still bleeding, even though it was probably icy cold and even Hugh's teeth were chattering from the cold. Somehow he managed to straighten the General's mangled leg and cut a couple of sturdy saplings, which he strapped around the mangled leg tied with strips of cloth cut from his own tunic and coat, while he tried to remember what he had been taught about the human skeleton and to arrange the leg in what he thought was the correct bone position. Thinking all the time that they needed to find somewhere he could warm the general up and try to find some food for them both, otherwise they would certainly die from exposure as it was now nearing midwinter, he realised that the rivers would soon freeze and the snow would be thick on the ground, so shelter and warmth and then food was the first priority. Despite the cold and all his pains, he lay down and slept and awoke to find the sky was not night and a beam of sunlight was dazzling his eyes and it was the day after the battle, yet here they were the only survivors of the once proud 9th Legion of the greatest empire in the world. He saw that the general was still alive although he was breathing very very faintly. As he looked around he saw there was a small shack just visible in the woods. He managed with what seemed his last bit of strength to pull the general into the shelter, where he was most surprised to find a pile of firewood and a couple of blankets. He immediately wrapped around the General while he started to light a fire. He began to feel his body warm up again and finally he was able to move around and, as he heard the General coughing he realised that he must now leave him and find some food. This was not at all difficult, as there were plenty of large fish swimming up the river and they were quite easy to catch with his bare hands and were killed by smashing their heads on the rock. He then went about gutting the fish and then cutting them into strips, which he grilled on the fire, although some he allowed to dry smoke. The General's eyes fluttered open and the General spoke in little more than a whisper, "What is happening? Where are we? What happened?"

"Just eat this General, everything will be fine, don't worry about anything else just yet. You concentrate on getting some food inside you, I will explain everything later," said Hugh trying to sound optimistic and jovial. With that he fell into an exhausted sleep himself.

*   *   *   *   *

Rosanna was happy with her new job and went into labour about fifteen days after the winter solstice, right at the beginning of the New Year. She gave birth without much difficulty, and found that she had a fine son, who she decided to call Petros, even though the name was Greek, the Romans seemed to favour many of the Greek customs and were even adopting the Greek language, instead of their own language, now known as Latin. Petros was a sturdy baby, who looked like his father, but had the same eyes as Rosanna, which were green, but without the golden highlights. Rosanna was very keen to write and tell Hugh about his son, that she would name Petros, which translated to 'The Rock'. She did not know then that this was the name that Christ had given to the leader of his disciples, the man who was later to come to Rome and be crucified upside down, just outside the city. She also never realised that Christianity would play a very large part in their future lives.

When Rosanna was feeding her baby the next morning, she heard a commotion outside in the main living area. It was Senator Latitch, with his customary bodyguards, who had forced their way into the room and were proudly announcing that the 9th Legion had been obliterated. This they announced with great pleasure knowing that it would infuriate Cynthia, General Priam's sister. Senator Latitch went on to announce, "Do not worry yourself Miss Priam, even though you have lost your main financial supporter, I will buy the wives of the soldiers of the 9th Legion, they can act as my serving maids at some of the parties that I have for many of the Senators, particularly when we need support for a new idea that has to gain legislation," he chuckled. He looked around at the frightened faces, because they all knew that his parties were orgies, where many of the serving girls were expected to entertain their guests, displaying their bodies and offering themselves as play things.

As Senator Latitch left with his two accompanying bodyguards, amongst all the concerned faces, Cynthia Priam was the first to recover. She made her way over to Rosanna and put her arm around Rosanna's shoulders to comfort her, as she seemed to be in dire distress. "Try not to worry Rosanna, I will keep you here as long as I can. I feel sure that something will turn up to save you from Senator Latitch, so try and not worry," she said consolingly. Despite the kind words from Cynthia Priam, Rosanna could not help being concerned, not only for herself and the baby but also because of Hugh, he certainly did not deserve this and she felt certain that he was still alive. Could the information that Senator Latitch had spoken about be incorrect? Unfortunately he was a Senator, but was he always correct? Surely not, she thought, but a tiny voice in the back of her head told her that the 9th Legion had been destroyed, and that Queen Boadicea was marching towards Londinium.

Over the next twenty days Rosanna tried not to worry, but many of the other wives of soldiers who had served in the 9th Legion were also worried, particularly her friend Lydia who was also very attractive and they spent a lot of her free time together, when she was not demonstrating her language skills and teaching. Their troubles were renewed when Senator Latitch returned and said that he would take the wives of the soldiers from the 9th Legion. He strutted over to Rosanna and Lydia and said, "I will take these two first. I will send a few bodyguards to collect them in three days time." With that he strutted back out of Senator Priam's house, chuckling loudly to himself, making sure that all could see and hear him and obviously tremble at his words.

*   *   *   *   *

Hugh woke early the next morning and took a few moments to realise where he was. The General was lying next to the fire, which had almost burnt out, but there were still some glowing embers left, which Hugh managed to blow into a fire, which he fed with more wood, until the fire was crackling again and spreading some warmth around them. Hugh could see that the General was breathing by the slow rise and fall of his chest. He leaned across and felt the General's face, it was warm and at his light touch the General's eyes fluttered open. Hugh spoke to the General, "Good morning, Sir. How does your leg feel? I am afraid that it was broken, but I bound it up and put splints either side of the break, so I have every confidence that it will heal properly and you will be able to walk again." Hugh knew the General too well, but hoped that he sounded hopeful and that the General would not despair at the loss of his legion.

"Thank you, Hugh, for all that you have done for me, all I can remember of the fight is that we were driven back up and then my horse reared and Queen Boadicea charging at me, it must have been one of her chariot wheels that ran over my leg, at least I was not cut to ribbons by the knives on the chariot's wheels. However, tell me what happened in the battle." He looked around and saw that they were alone and before Hugh could offer any sort of explanation, he answered his own question. "The legion is destroyed, are we the only survivors?"

"I am afraid we are, but I do not know exactly where we are. You see my knowledge of Britain is not very extensive, although I did look at some maps that were in York, I do not know which river we are beside, yet they all lead to the sea, where we can try to steal a boat and I can sail us back south to Londinium, if that is still standing."

"I should imagine that it is, Hugh. Queen Boadicea may have raided most of the tribes in northern Britain, but she will not have been able to take Londinium, so I think we had better stick to your plan. There are many small rivers that lead down to the sea north of York, but I am afraid that I am not exactly sure where we are, because the maps are not clear, although it cannot be far. So I am sorry to be a burden on you, all I can promise is that if you can return us to Londinium, I will certainly reward you and promote you to being a Centurion!"

Hugh chuckled and said, "Just leave everything to me, Sir, you eat some of this fish that I smoked over the fire last night and leave the rest to me." He knew that he was trying to sound more confident than he felt but he was sure that he could build a raft and with luck manage to get them to the coast, where there were bound to be some fishermen.

He had to leave the General for a while, so he told him that he would be back soon, but that the General should not make too much noise as he was not sure that there was nobody else in the vicinity. So he set off creeping quietly through the trees, grateful that this was a fir forest and all the needles on the ground muffled his footsteps. Although he saw a fox and a few red squirrels, he saw nothing else, even though he made a fairly good expedition around the immediate vicinity. He saw nothing to alarm him, except the deep claw marks that had been made fairly recently by a bear. He knew that the bears liked the fish from the river, so he did not wait long before he returned to General Priam with a few birds eggs that he had found in a nest. He was not sure what bird had laid the eggs, although he was sure that they were fresh and that they would make a nice change to their diet of fish. He then went about building a raft from the large dead trees that he found near by, cutting the thick logs into more manageable lengths, which he dragged over to where the General was lying. Leaving the General with plenty of wood for the fire, he made his way back to the battlefield, in the hope of finding rope or anything that would assist him in building a raft. He knew that this would be a grisly task, because most of the Iceni women had butchered the dead Roman soldiers and had probably plundered any supplies that might have been remaining, still he walked off massaging his aching right arm, trying to remember when he had ached so much, particularly in his right arm from using his dagger to cut the logs.

He eventually came out of the fir forest, which gradually turned into deciduous trees, and followed the river upstream, eventually emerging onto the battlefield. He was quite surprised that he had managed to take the General as far away as he had done, yet he was correct in that the work was very grim. Not only had the dead Romans been cut up into pieces, but their bodies had been half burnt, nearly all of the provisions had been ransacked and most things of any use had been taken. Although after a lot of searching he came across some rope, as well as some medical supplies, which he supposed the Iceni had no knowledge of, so had discarded. Feeling very pleased with his finds, he made his way back down the river to find the General, who was yelling at something, and at which he was throwing flaming bits of wood. Hugh had to duck as one of the Generals firebrands whistled over his head, so he called out, "Its alright General, its only me and I've found what I was looking for, with an unforeseen bonus." He put down everything he had been gathering and showed them to General Priam, who was delighted at seeing the medical supplies, explaining that he had been throwing the fire brands at the wolves, that had been attracted by the smell of blood. Hugh told him that he had seen many of the creatures around the battlefield, although he was glad that he did not see the bear that had made the deep gouges in the trees, as it was obviously a very large bear, but it had probably satiated its appetite on the many dead soldiers. He had also found a couple of shallow pans, that he put on the fire and then he boiled some water,

53

into which he poured some antiseptic liquid and cleaned the General's leg up, before rebinding it better. He then worked about building the raft, using the rope and all his skill that he learned in the army or even before when he was a gladiator, as well as his previous skills as a fisherman. Hugh worked for the rest of the daylight hours and then caught another large fish that was swimming up river. It was exhausted, so that probably indicated that there were some rapids or waterfalls down river. He was very pleased to find that the General was in a more agreeable mood; he had started to cook some of the fish before saying to Hugh,

"You have done very well lad, I feel that we will manage to get back to Londinium, even though it is still a lot of work for you, because of this damned injury of mine." Hugh and the General made sure that the fire was burning well and discussed their plans to find a boat, because the General was sure that his charts had marked a town near the coast on this very river. The General stayed awake most of the night, while Hugh lay in exhausted sleep. It was not until the grey light of dawn when the General shook Hugh by the shoulder saying, "Wake up lad, I don't think that there is any danger but one of us should try to keep awake and although it is a shame to wake you, I cannot keep my eyes open for much longer."

"Gosh, is it the next day already? You really should have woken me earlier, you must be very tired."

"Well I suppose I am, but you are doing all the work, so you need more sleep, apart from which I am older than you I do not need so much sleep." Yet as he said this, his eyes closed and he was fast asleep. Hugh finished what he had been working on the previous day, before starting to cook some more fish, he then woke the General and they ate in companiable silence, preparing for the next leg of their journey.

Despite Hugh's earlier misgivings, it only took one and a half days to reach a broader river, where there was a town, just as the General had predicted. This was nothing more than a small village and by the look of the village, it was mainly home to local fisher folk who generally did not become involved in tribal or territorial battles, they simply lived on the fish that they caught and raised their children in the same way that their parents had brought them up. Fortunately, Hugh and the General were becoming very close friends now, and saw the village by its cooking fires as they came to it at night. Hugh made the raft secure, by tying it to a tree near the riverbank, before walking around to reconnoitre the village, when he came across a small flock of sheep that were secured in a crude pen. He quickly stunned one of the lambs and carried it to the General, thinking that it would make a nice change of diet, as well as the pelt being useful. He was sure that he could skin the animal quite successfully; his old backwoods skills were returning to him. He managed to quieten some of the village dogs that started yapping and snarling, as they were trained for that very purpose. This he did by throwing them chunks of cooked or dried fish and found then they became quite placid.

Hugh found the type of boat that he was looking for; it was very similar to the type of boat that he used to use. It was conveniently moored slightly apart from the other boats on the river. After checking that it was equipped with oars and a good sail, he was also pleased to realise that it was well-equipped with fishing lines. He untied the boat and rowed it to where the General was waiting, fortunately this was not very far. The General looked up in surprise, and said, "Goodness me Hugh, you were remarkably quick. You obviously know a lot about fishing boats!"

"Well Sir, it is quite strange, but it is all coming back to me, just as if I had never stopped fishing, many things that I used to do are now returning to me, as if joining the army and being a gladiator had never happened." He made the boat secure, by tying the fore and aft painters to a convenient tree trunk and root, which were growing near to where the General was lying. He jumped lightly ashore and went over to where the General was sitting up and helped him into the boat, making sure that he was sitting as comfortably as possible and was right in the middle of the boat with both hands around the mast. "Here we go General!" They were just in time, as one of the dogs began to growl. Unbeknown to Hugh they had just stolen the dog's master's boat, which was why the dog became agitated, as he could not understand the strange behaviour of these two men. Keeping the boat in midstream, he used the oars as little as possible so that he would not make any splashing sounds that might awaken one of the village's fishermen. Hugh watched the village drift past and did not start rowing until they were well out of hearing range. He then bent to the oars with a will, trying to put as much distance between them and the village before dawn. Much to Hugh's delight, he saw a much larger settlement, just as the sky was beginning to light up in the east, the direction that they were heading. Some other fishermen were boarding their own boats here and one of them called out to Hugh. It was a dialect that he could not easily understand, although the meaning was quite clear. The other man was simply saying that they must have left early, so Hugh simply shouted back "Aye, that we did." He had tried to make his voice sound as if he came from the north of Britain, to make the other men think that he was local, simply leaving only to make a full day fishing. He was obviously successful as there was no reply, the other man simply went back to what he had been doing. Hugh could smell the sea air, as he remembered the fresh salty smell, indicating that they were nearing the coast. In addition there was a slight breeze blowing on his back.

The light breeze was a fairly normal off-shore wind, a normal feature for the east coast of Britain, although Hugh did not know the name of the main river that he was now drifting and paddling down. It was the River Tyne and as he was swept around the next bend, he could even hear the surf breaking on the seashore, as well as the island, which was later called Lindisfarne. Hugh rowed the boat and then shipped the oars as he stood up to raise the sail. When he could see the wind in the sail he put the tiller into its socket at the stern of the boat and steered well to the south of Lindisfarne. The water was very clear, although quite cold and he could see other small boats like his emerging from the river and lifting to the swell of the sea. Like Hugh, they steered to the south of the island, as if he was directing them. He thought that this was very strange and realised that he had to move away from the normal fishing fleet, so that he was on his own. Therefore he started rowing again and soon the other boats began throwing out their fishing nets, as there were plenty of surface fish, like mackerel and herring. He was now at least one thousand cubits ahead of the main fleet, who paid no attention to him, thinking correctly that he was going somewhere different. The weather helped them, as they went further away, and as the bows lifted to a large wave Hugh could see that the sky to the north looked very stormy. He said to the General, "I think we are in for a bit of a blow, but it will take us in the right direction, we need to head south. However, will you keep a watch on the shore, as we may need to keep well away from any boats or obstacles that may be in the way, you see I have no knowledge of the coast this far north."

"Aye aye, Captain," grinned the General! This was a sign of the friendship that had developed between them, so they kept on all day moving before the wind. Towards evening, Hugh decided to head towards the shore, as it would be very dangerous to risk being blown well out to sea, particularly as there were no stars to guide them, so they came ashore well to the North of most of the small villages near the River Humber, where it flowed into the sea. They had plenty of food with them, with the smoked fish and the fresh lamb, although Hugh knew that they really needed some wheat or some roots to mix their diet. Hugh pulled the boat ashore, realising how cold the water was as he jumped over the side. He had been keeping himself warm by all the exercise of rowing the boat and he realised that the General must be cold, even though he had not complained. Hugh managed to light a small fire having cut some dead branches off a few trees and left the General for a while, who was trying to warm himself and roast some of the lamb that Hugh had butchered. Hugh was lucky finding some freshly laid eggs, that must have just been laid by a sea bird, as they were slightly speckled but were in a very hastily scraped nest in the sand. He looked around and found some nuts, taking these back with the eggs to the General. They feasted together and talked about what they were going to do tomorrow, not realising that many miles inland Queen Boadicea was running all the British tribes and attempting to throw the Romans out of Britain.

They awoke early the next morning and Hugh lifted the General back into the boat and pushed the boat into the sea, before climbing in himself and rowing back southwards yet keeping fairly near to the shore. This morning he threw out some fishing lines that were not weighted, but had some meat on the fishhooks, to try and tempt the surface fish. Again Hugh was amazed at the General's strength of character, as he never complained at all, but left all the decisions to Hugh. This made it a lot easier as Hugh could keep an eye on the fishing lines and also a close watch on the shore to their right as they passed the mouth of the River Humber and the Wash when they had to turn more to the south east. This was where the Romans were digging clay from the large pits, by using many British slaves, this area was later to be named the Norfolk Broads. They continued until Hugh could steer the boat directly south, and they had caught a couple of fish, which the General pulled on board and killed by knocking the fish on their heads, so that they died quickly. They took the boat towards the shore again and Hugh once more beached the boat and they sat around the fire trying to keep themselves warm, even though Hugh was not as cold as the General had been, yet this evening when Hugh left the General for a while he was not as successful with his foraging. Still, Hugh thought that he was nearing some of the lands that he knew and he mentioned this to the General saying, "Hopefully we will reach the River Thames soon, Sir, from where we can row into Londinium."

"If it is still there, my boy," replied the General. This was what Hugh had been thinking, but he did not wish to sound pessimistic, because he wanted to be able to return to see Rosanna, who had probably had their baby. He wanted to be able to reassure her that he and the General were safe, as well as of course seeing the baby. They fairly soon saw a distant Roman galley leaving from the east, it was riding high in the water, showing that it had very little on board, so they surmised that it had brought more troops to Londinium. Hugh now had to lower the sail and row up the River Thames, feeling grateful they would soon reach civilisation and the General could receive the medical attention that he needed. It was a very tired Hugh who caught the mooring line, that was thrown out by one of the sailors on the shore in the city of Londinium.

Part Two

"Home to Rome"

The dreadful day had finally arrived, Rosanna had just finished feeding Petros, who was a fairly easy baby to care for, as he slept well at night. For this she was grateful and it gave her a good night sleep. Lydia remarked on this as well, praising the child, as did Cynthia Priam. Rosanna had just finished adjusting her tunic when the hated voice of Senator Latitch was heard. "Good day to you lovely ladies, I feel sure that you are very keen to come and work for me, ha ha ha," he chuckled, seeing the look of horror on their faces. He came over to Rosanna and said, "I trust that brat has not sucked you dry." He then answered his own question by saying, "It appears not, you appear quite well rounded." Then to Rosanna's horror he squeezed her breast and smilingly remarked, "I will be holding one of my gatherings very soon, my Senator friends all like to see my new serving girls." He then turned as another messenger arrived from the Emperor. He stood in shocked disbelief as the messenger spoke loudly to Cynthia Priam.

"Good news madam, we have just received a message from Londinium. The uprising in Britain has just been checked north of Londinium, your brother the General was the only survivor of the 9th Legion, well him and one of his centurions, who managed to row him back to the capital where he is receiving medical attention, because his leg was badly broken by Queen Boadacea's chariot. The centurion, who is a man called Hugh, managed to escape from the battle which destroyed the 9th Legion. They have both written scrolls to you, as I knew you are looking after the centurion's wife, but all that is here for you to read." He gave the scrolls to Cynthia Priam, simply nodded his recognition to the Senator and added, "They are treating him like a hero, I suppose this is strange, because he lost a legion, although the Emperor Nero is asking for him to be returned to Rome and honoured, as well as promoting the centurion who brought him back." With a contemptuous smile at the disbelieving look on the Senator's face he left.

Nobody moved at first, although Cynthia Priam came to her senses first, and said to Senator Latitch, "You and your rascals will leave immediately and don't dare enter this house again, for if you do I will make use of the General's weapons," adding as she approached the Senator with one of his swords that she had taken from the wall, which she drew from its scabbard, making a slightly rasping whisper, a fearful and threatening noise. "I will take great pleasure in chopping off your balls and also your prick, so that you will have to squat to piss, you bastard." Senator made a hasty departure, but threw back over his shoulder,

"I always thought that Nero was mad."

Nobody said anything for quite a long time, as none of the girls had ever seen Cynthia Priam in such a bad temper before. To be honest they never wanted to see her in such a mood again, or certainly not being on the receiving end, as she obviously meant exactly what she said. It was generally accepted by many Romans that the Emperor Nero was very strange, although nobody normally said such a thing, as to do so was considered an act of treason.

* * * * *

Hugh slept very well and was pleased that he was allowed to wake of his own accord, rather than being shaken awake, or woken by a bugle blast. He was grateful to be in a civilised place and to be rested well, before being treated like an honoured guest by the Roman soldiers who were also looking after General Priam. They had tended his leg with skill, although the principal doctor was most concerned and had told Hugh, out of the General's hearing, "You did a very fine job in bringing him back to me here, but I do not think the bones will ever correctly mend themselves in the normal way, because it was what we call a complicated fracture. You see my boy, when his leg was broken it was not a clean break, but there must have been a lot of small pieces of bone in the fracture."

"Do you mean that he will never walk again," asked Hugh.

"Oh no, that is not what I mean," replied the doctor. "What I am suggesting, is that he will probably not be able to walk without limping, and will certainly not run again."

"Well that is alright," replied Hugh. "Because as he is a General, he will either ride astride a horse or stand in a chariot."

"Well, we will just have to wait and see, but I believe the General wants to see you and there is no time like the present, so let us go back and see him." The doctor took Hugh to where the General was in bed, being rude to all the orderlies and staff who came in, as he wanted to be out of bed. The doctor came within speaking distance. "General Priam, I have brought the centurion who brought you here, I believe that you wanted to see him." The doctor then made a hasty retreat, leaving Hugh alone with the General.

"I believe you wanted to see me General," said Hugh.

"Yes Hugh, I want to reward you and promote you to being a Tribuni, which I will do as soon as the damn quack lets me out of here!"

"Thank you, Sir," replied Hugh awkwardly. "But I was only doing my duty."

"Rubbish, boy. Without your help I would have died on the battlefield, with the rest of the 9th Legion." As Hugh left, the General called and said, "Send that doctor back to me. I trust that you are being treated well, as you are being promoted to a Tribune. That will give you a lot more influence, so I will expect great things of you in the future."

"Gosh, thank you, Sir, that is a great promotion, I will certainly try not to let you down. I will go and find the doctor now. Will it be alright if I write to Rosanna and let her know the good news?" said Hugh and realised that he was blushing.

"Of course you can, my boy, you will also need a new uniform, so I will send the tailors to see you," was the General's final remark.

The doctor then returned and whispered to Hugh as they passed, "It will be easily another ten days before we can allow the General to leave and even then, his leg will be in splints, making it impossible for him to put any weight on his injured leg. Still, he is alive and I believe that he will be given a new legion to command." Hugh made his way back to his own quarters, still unable to believe his good fortune. He thought he had better spend as much time as possible in reading up on the duties that he would have to provide, because he obviously wanted to make a success of his new job.

He spent the next several days reading about the duties of a Tribuni, although he did not neglect his normal few hours of sword practice, as well as general weapon training, to keep himself quite fit. He also took to running around the city walls, carrying increasingly heavier weights to ensure that he kept himself in prime condition. He made many new friends in Londinium, but none of them came as close to him as his friends in the 9th Legion, or even his old friend Adobe, when he had trained as a gladiator. He even went swimming occasionally across the River Thames and most of the soldiers and even sailors thought he was slightly crazy as it was still early in the year and the water was not warm. Mind you, nobody said anything to his face, as they all admired and respected him for his achievement in rescuing General Priam. They could also see how fit and strong he was so they would not wish to be rude to him, but would offer him goblets of wine or encourage him to play dice with them or take part in other evening pursuits, which were most enjoyable. The only thing Hugh did not join in was visiting one of the many brothels that some of his new friends went to, as some of the women folk were not very attractive and there was also the danger of catching a disease. When he was visited by the tailor, who took all his measurements, the tailor remarked, "You are very fit and well built, I have been ordered to make you a uniform using the finest linen cloth that will look splendid, so please do not get it covered with blood from the many enemies that you will kill." Hugh wrote to Rosanna, telling her about his promotion and new uniform, additionally enquiring about their new baby, which he had heard was a boy and that she had named him Petros, wondering why she had chosen a Greek name. When he told the General this, the General told him that Greek was becoming a more commonly used language and it was a far better language as there were a lot more verbs than other parts of speech, which made it easier to express oneself. He also advised Hugh that it would be an advantage for him to learn the language, because it might well become the main language used by the Romans. So this was another duty that Hugh had to accomplish and he wished that his two friends from Rodos were still with him and could help him with his studies, although the librarian was Greek and helped him with the studies and that would eventually prove very useful.

Eventually General Priam was released from the hospital and insisted on attending to a few light duties, assisting the Governor of Londinium in exercising some of his troops. When Hugh's new uniform was ready, a date was arranged for his promotion. This was carried out in front of the entire garrison in the new auditorium. Hugh had been here before as a spectator, it seated over two thousand and he had been here to watch a gladiators' fight, that he considered was poor sport, compared to the standard that he had been used to in Gaul, expected by Aurolius. He had also watched some bear baiting, when a large brown bear was chained to an iron ring attached to a stake, where it was attacked by a pack of savage wolves that were kept for the very purpose of attacking a bear, which was not their normal prey. The crowd seemed to love this sport, although Hugh thought it was ridiculous entertainment and very unfair on the poor bear, which was torn to pieces. In fact the only sport that Hugh enjoyed in the auditorium was the chariot racing, although the crowd seemed to enjoy violent sports and plenty of bloodshed, particularly when a prisoner was brought into the arena and was sentenced to death by being torn to pieces by wild animals or being beheaded by a large axe man. Hugh had already written to Rosanna, saying that he would be promoted and was awaiting her reply. He hoped she would be very pleased and should expect that he would be returning to Rome with General Priam as a Tribune, and that she would need to dress accordingly, as well as entertaining any guests who called to see him officially.

He did not have long to wait and realised that she must have written her reply immediately, it certainly looked as if she had written very quickly, without checking on the spelling as some of the words were hastily written and even the ink had been smudged. Her letter basically said that she was delighted that he and the General were safe and were coming back to Rome where she would be delighted to see him and show him their baby, whom she had decided to call Petros. He realised that she had possibly kept the delivery person waiting while she wrote the letter. Hugh knew that he was very keen to see the new baby and knew that Rosanna would be a very good hostess, in fact he realised that he would have many people who would come just to see his beautiful wife and he could almost picture the scene, with him introducing his lovely wife to many soldier friends and possibly politicians or people with influence with the Emperor. This in turn made him think of Senator Latitch, this was not a pleasant thought, and although Rosanna had not mentioned Senator Latitch, he was sure that the evil little pot bellied hangman's dilemma knew about his wife, that she was living with General Priam's sister and that her omission of Senator Latitch by name was possibly deliberate! Hugh decided that he would speak to General Priam, and ask whether or not his sister had any dealings with Senator Latitch, who was someone that Hugh was beginning to fear, not for himself, but for Rosanna and Petros. He was not personally afraid of the Senator, in fact very few people worried him, but was concerned about Rosanna and the baby.

The very next day Hugh made time to see General Priam, who was always very pleased to see him.

"Good morning my boy," said the general, as he stopped writing. "You look worried, is there anything I can do?"

"Yes General, you see, I have received a letter from Rosanna." Hugh finished speaking as the general held up his hand.

"I know what is worrying you, it is Senator Latitch," replied the general. "Do I guess correctly?"

"Yes, sir you do," replied Hugh, quite surprised that the general knew.

"You see, I have received a letter from my sister, telling me all about the Senator and his last visit, apparently she threatened do cut his balls off," the general laughed. I wish that I had been there to watching, my sister has quite a temper, she is someone not to cross."

"I am glad that she is in safe hands," replied Hugh. "However have you any idea how much longer we will have to wait here, because I will not feel really happy until I can see my wife and the baby?"

"Yes Hugh, I obviously appreciate your feelings, which I share. I am concerned for my sister and all the ladies in the house, so I share your concerns. Yes, we will be leaving soon, the doctor has given me permission to travel back to Rome, soon we will be on the next galley that will return us home."

It was about five days later when a galley docked at the wharf. As soon as they disembarked the troops and the cargo was unloaded from the holds. Hugh ran up the gangplank and went to find the captain. "When will you be ready to return to Rome, Captain?"

The captain, who was a short swarthy man, replied, "To be honest we have had a very difficult journey, particularly the last few days. What is that large bay on Gaul called?"

"Oh yes," exclaimed Hugh, "That is called the Bay of Biscay, the weather in autumn is often very bad there!"

"Yes, by the gods, I thought we were going to sink, it is very treacherous," the captain agreed.

"However Captain I did not come to ask about your journey here," Hugh pressed on determined to finish. "What I really wanted to know was how soon you will be ready to return to Rome?"

The captain spoke to Hugh, but Hugh pretended that he had not heard. "I am asking when you will be returning, so that I can bring General Priam on board."

"Well, the great General," he looked at Hugh with new respect, almost with awe. "I suppose that we will be returning in about five or maybe six days time, it will depend on how soon we can load the goods we have to take back with us."

"Alright Captain, I am sure that I can try to speed things up for you," as Hugh looked at the exhausted slaves, who looked in very poor condition. He simply said, "As soon as you feel your slaves have recovered." Hugh knew that General Priam would understand, as the general was a decent man, who respected slaves and knew that they had their own problems.

Hugh went to see the General, although he did not want the General to interfere, trusting that the General would let him make the arrangements. He found the General in the library, surrounded by scrolls; he was working on new military tactics. He looked up at Hugh and said, "Yes Hugh, you look slightly worried, is there anything troubling you?"

"Not really General," replied Hugh, "It is simply that a galley just arrived and will be returning to Rome, but the Captain said that he needs at least five or six days before we could return to Rome. To be honest I think that he was being overoptimistic."

"I understand my boy," replied the General, "I expect that you were worried about the slaves on the rowing benches."

"Yes General I was, and I think that 8 to 10 days would be a more realistic forecast."

"All right, that is fine," said the General

Hugh sighed with relief. "You see I would like to return to Rome as soon as possible, but I suppose a few extra days will not really matter, in fact it would give you time to finish what you are working on."

"Yes, you are perfectly correct, I am just working on how a siege should be organised. You see, we have captured many towns and cities over the past few years, but there has often been a lot of unnecessary bloodshed, which we must stop because it makes it a lot more difficult to control the people."

"Therefore I suggest you go back to tell the captain that we are in no rush, a few extra days will be fine and he should allow his slaves plenty of time to rest."

"I will do that immediately Sir," responded Hugh. He paused for a moment, "Would you allow me to read the new instruction, sir?"

"Most certainly, my boy, as soon as you have delivered my message to the captain!"

As Hugh returned he read the general's instructions and discussed a few ideas he had himself. Eventually he spent quite a few days working and went to the general, it certainly helped to fill up the next few days and made Hugh realise that there was a great deal of wisdom the General was writing. He realised that people often have different beliefs, worshipped different gods, that it should be allowed and not interfered with because people were quite happy to be ruled, particularly if they were given the opportunity to change the rules themselves in a democratic way. This activity kept him from worrying about Rosanna and the baby and the final few nights were spent in enjoyable discussion and in finishing the new instructions.

Hugh and the General were in the middle of a discussion, when the captain of the galley came to see them. He said "There you are. I have been looking for you everywhere, but I suppose that I should have realised that you would be working in here. Anyway, I have come to inform you that all the provisions are now on board and the crew is all rested, so what we are now waiting for is you. When will you be ready to join us?"

Hugh looked at the general, who also looked at Hugh, as he said to the captain, "I am sorry that we have not been ready for you. Although it will only take us a few moments to be ready, is that not so?" Hugh asked the General.

The General said, "Yes, Captain, my tribune is correct and we are to blame for keeping you waiting. We can be ready to come on board tomorrow morning, basically everything is packed now and we have only to replace all the scroll that we have been using from the library," he waved his hand at all the empty scroll boxes.

"That will be excellent, General, I hope you do not object sharing a cabin together?"

"Certainly not Captain, I am sure that you have heard the story of how we escaped from the battle in Britain?"

There was a large crowd of people who came to watch the galley leave the next morning, it seemed like most of the people living in Londinium had come to watch. As it sailed down the river towards the sea, the general said to Hugh, "It is hard to believe that I lost a legion, it is more like they are saying farewell to a hero!"

"Well, that is the strange situation about warfare, the people will treat the Romans as conquerors today, but as plunderers tomorrow!"

The galley rowed away and turned south in between the newly extended empire of Rome that now stretched all the way from Britain in the northwest, to India in the south. Although not all countries had been subjugated, Hugh did not realise how prophetic his words were.

"Was it not around here, when I first met you Hugh?" asked the General.

"Well, it was certainly very near here sir. I used to go fishing in my small fishing boat from a village that was on marshlands just inland just a little further after the white cliffs. The village was called Rye in the British language, that can also mean a type of grass, which is used to make bread, or cakes," replied Hugh. They were standing on the quarterdeck just in front of the two large steering oars that were held by sailors, who kept them in position according to the directions given by the Captain. Hugh had previously brought his own gear on board, as well as the general's personal effects, and stowed them in the bedchamber next to where the Captain was sleeping when he was not on duty. The Captain always seemed to be on duty. When Hugh tried to work out the times that the duties changed, he was told that the duties on board a galley were worked out in different ways, they changed according to the number of times a bell was sounded. This seemed very unusual to Hugh and he wondered why the sailors could not use a simple system like that used in the army. He found this very confusing and asked the General why, but was told that the sailors considered their service to be senior to the army. By the look on the General's face, this was a mystery to him, so Hugh did not pursue the subject any further. He simply shrugged his shoulders, and looked at the general in despair.

The galley continued gradually journeying east, until they could see the coast of Gaul faraway on the left, while the oars rose and fell, rose and fell, in a hypnotic rhythm. Hugh realised that he had been standing and watching the oars for quite a long time, as if he had fallen under their spell, and suddenly he realised that the General was repeating the same question, "I asked if you know what the weather will be like at this time of the year?"

"I am sorry Sir, I must have been dreaming, you see it is just the rhythm of the oars. I am sure that you wanted to ask me something very important, would you be good enough to repeat your question?"

The general laughed, "I realised that, it is quite understandable, I have seen many people do exactly the same. However as you are familiar with this area, do you know what type of weather we can expect?"

"Well it can be quite calm, although it can change very quickly, particularly at this time of the year. You see the water is not very deep here and at times you get to see the sea bed, or occasionally when there is a very low tide you often see mud flats."

"What do you mean by that, tide?" asked the General.

"It is what we call the depth of the water, it changes at least twice a day. Although I cannot explain why, there are many people who have different ideas, some of them are quite reasonable, but others are rather strange. It seems to be that we have still a lot to find out about the world we live in."

"Yes my boy, in the sea we are going to, it is very different, and the Greeks had many strange stories about the monsters in the water, although I have never seen anything larger than a shark."

"How large was that, sir?"

"It was about as long as I am, but I believe that they can be very large. I know many people who have seen much larger fish than I have and they are responsible people, not people who are telling stories."

"I have seen some very large sharks, but they did not seem to be dangerous to us. I suppose that we will learn a lot more as we study the fish in the sea, Hugh." They stood in companionable silence until it started to become dark, when they decided to go to their cabin below the deck, where they would be warmer. Hugh then asked the General a question about something that he had recently heard. "Have you heard anything about a group of people who call themselves Christians?"

"Yes Hugh, I have heard," replied the General thoughtfully, "but I must warn you, it is not a belief that the Emperor likes, so it should be treated with care. I do not think that it is very wise to believe in anything that might offend the Emperor or his senators." They then discussed the new duties that Hugh would have, provided that the General was given a new legion to command. After a while they went to bed.

Early the next morning Hugh was woken up as the galley was pitching quite violently, although the general was still fast asleep, but Hugh had never been a person who liked lying in bed, and he went to see if he could arrange any breakfast. He dressed and left the cabin to see what was happening. When he arrived on deck he found that the galley was still sailing, even in a very high wind, and that was the main reason for the motion on the galley. He knew that in this wind they really should slow down, by shortening the sail, by reefing it or taking down the sail completely and running before the wind and steering the galley, while the rowers rested on their oars. Hugh thought that he should have a talk with the captain, but was told the captain was not in charge on the galley at the moment. "Well, who is in charge at the moment?" demanded Hugh.

"One of his boatswains, sir!"

"Show me where he is, because he will do some damage to the galley. I will tell him he is crazy, as this a very silly way to manage a galley."

A short man said to Hugh, "What is the problem Tribune? I was told by the captain to reach the opening to the inland sea, as soon as possible."

Realising that he had to do something very quickly, Hugh went to find the captain, but when he reached the captain's cabin he was told by one of his senior sailors that the captain was unwell and had given instructions that he was not to be disturbed. Hugh knew that all the crew on board the galley had more respect for the General than they had for their own captain, so he went to wake the General. When he went into the General's cabin, he found that the General was already awake.

"What is happening, Hugh?" asked the General.

"Well, the Captain is not well and the Boatswain who is in charge of steering the galley will not listen to me, so I thought that you could use your authority, as they all respect you and will do whatever you wish," he explained.

"No problem Hugh, I will be right with you," said the General as he quickly dressed and followed Hugh onto deck. As they emerged on deck, one glance from the General was all he needed and he shouted

"Who is temporarily in charge. By the gods, what are you trying to do?" All the sailors looked at him, in complete surprise. "Are you trying to dismast the galley, or tear the sail to ribbons, because if you are, you are doing a damn good job!"

The offending officer looked abashed and stammered, "I, I was only following orders, sir."

"Shorten the sails and just run the galley before the wind." The sailors took some reefs in the sail. This was done just as the seams began to pop, but the galley immediately stopped pitching like a mad runaway horse. "Now listen to what my tribune tells you, I am leaving him in charge, is that understood?" The General turned and said, "You are now in charge and if anyone disputes your orders I give you permission to chop their heads off and feed them to the fish." This was said above the noise of the wind. "Now I am going to speak to the Captain and tell him what is going on."

Hugh went over to speak quietly to the officer who had received the full fury of the General's words, "Please do not worry, I am not trying to take over the galley, it is just that I needed someone to listen to what I was trying to tell you, you see I was originally a fisherman, please let us be friends". He then held out his hand, which was taken and everybody smiled in friendship.

Some time later the general returned and was obviously pleased to see that everybody was working in harmony. He smiled at Hugh and said, "You seem to have a good understanding of people. I demanded to the see the Captain, who was simply overworking himself, although I think he will be alright provided that he rests. Does anyone know where we are?"

"Well Sir," replied Hugh, "I believe that we are South of Gaul now and I think that the land that you can see to the left is called Iberia, or Spain in the British language. Hopefully if we keep going with this following wind, we will soon reach the entrance to the inland sea, or what they call the Pillars of Hercules." Hugh paused for a moment and then asked, "Why are they called that Sir?"

"To be honest Hugh, I often wondered that myself, it is a strange name, is it not?" The question was purely rhetorical as the General continued speaking. "You see we simply inherited the name from the Greeks, who actually called that strong man Hercules! To the north the entrance is marked by a huge rock but the southern shore is quite normal, although the sea inside is very nice, particularly in the summer. I do not think that we ever had any experience of the violent storms that are more common in your country." The wind gradually died and the sail was raised again and it was pleasant sailing, although on the right the sun went behind a dark cloud, showing that there might be a storm further out to the west. They ate some fruit and bread while they discussed some of the campaigns that the General had been in, mainly south of the inland sea where he described a huge sandy desert, which sounded so incredible that Hugh thought the General was elaborating or at least possibly exaggerating. Hugh could not envisage such a place, and then the General told him about the enormous river with many mouths, each one being larger than the river Londonium is on. They finally went below deck and the General was telling Hugh about a land called Judea, which was at the end of the Inland Sea.

Hugh was very interested to hear about this country, as the General seemed to think that there was a good chance of him going out there, where there were some problems with the people, who had a strange belief in having only one God, rather than the Pantheon of gods whom the Romans worshipped just like the Greeks before them, or even the Egyptians before them. Hugh eventually asked the General, "What do you believe in Sir?"

The General drew his sword, "That is what I believe in, but it must be used with care, you see all the Gods that are worshipped only cause problems between different people."

Then Hugh finally understood what the General meant and why he had drafted his new instructions on how to rule a country. "Oh I understand. Do you really expect that we will be going there?"

"Yes, I think that I will be sent. You see the army has a way of rewarding its heroes, they send you somewhere more difficult," he grimaced. Judea has always been a difficult country to govern. I often wonder why we bothered to take it over, we have had nothing but trouble from the place. It is more trouble than it is worth. The people who live there are called Jews and they say that their land was given to them by their God and that it is a land of milk and honey."

"It sounds nice, but from your expression you do not agree with them?" Hugh asked.

"No, I certainly don't, it is a bloody awful small country and half of it is rocks or deserts and there is a lake that they call a sea, but it is so salty that you can not even swim in it. Everything around it dies, because there is no fresh water."

Hugh tried to imagine what type of country that was, it certainly did not sound somewhere that he would like to visit, but as the General had correctly said, when you were in the army you had to follow the orders that you were given and those orders were very often influenced by the wish of the Emperor who was often influenced by the Senate, which made Hugh think about Senator Latitch and he immediately felt uneasy.

The weather was fairly kind and by the next afternoon they docked in Gibraltar harbour, where Hugh looked at the huge rock of Gibraltar, which dwarfed the town and was larger than any rock face that Hugh had ever seen. He decided to go with the General to the shore where they would be able to have a hot meal and stretch their legs. The weather was nice and somehow this sky looked different, it was a different blue and seemed to be higher and more clear than the sky in Britain. He then looked at the small town on the southern shore, which was often called the gateway to Africa, where there were many fabulous and wonderful animals and mountains of gold, as well as enormous diamonds and other precious stones. It sounded too good to be true, like the stories that were told to children before they were put to bed.

Hugh walked down from the galley with the General and found that there was a party of senior officers who had come to meet the General. Hugh could see that the General was delighted at seeing so many of a community, his face lit up and he was soon shaking hands and introducing many new soldiers to Hugh, they were all either tribunes or senior officers. They directed the General and Hugh towards a dockside tavern, where many drinks were offered to the newcomers. At first the General launched into an account of his being thrown from his horse in the battle against Queen Boadicea and his rescue by Hugh. That made everybody look at Hugh with the new respect, but before anyone could say anymore Hugh held up his hands and silence fell on the party.

"The General had just promoted me from being a Senior Centurion into Tribune, so I simply did what I could, as the General is more than a commander to me, he is a friend. I know that in the army you should not show favouritism."

After a while the talk went to different matters such as family and friends and Hugh began to lose interest in the conversation and gazed at the huge slab of rock. He was sure that he could see small grey animals moving on the rock, but could not see how they could move on such a flat vertical surface. He therefore turned to the youngest Tribune who was possibly a few years older than himself and asked "Are those animals on the rock, or have I been drinking too much of this ouzo?"

The other Tribune laughed, "No, you have not been drinking too much. They are apes, that are only found here."

"What are apes?" asked a very surprised Hugh.

"They are an unusual type of monkey, somehow they manage to find something to grip on in the rock, it is a very weird sight. Some people have said that we are part of the same family, but I don't think that is the truth, with the possible exception of some of the Senators, or Tribune Harot."

Many of the others in the party had overheard this joke and they laughed, all except one man at the end who scowled. Hugh realised that this was Tribune Harot, who looked very strange. Even the General laughed, before he patted the man on the back.

"No way," said the General, "Nobody in the army is that bad! I am sure that Hugh was thinking about Senator Latitch, who condemned Hugh to die when Hugh was a gladiator." From then on the meeting became friendlier and Hugh even went to sit and talk to Tribune Harot. The General was offered quarters in Gibraltar, but said in a slightly slurred voice, "My friends we have excellent accommodation on board the galley." This was indeed a very kind thing to say, because a cabin was certainly not grand. Hugh stayed beside the General as they went back on board the galley, mainly to make sure that the General was alright and did not walk or stumble into anything that would damage his leg. When they were below deck again the General said to Hugh, "Thank you my boy, to be honest I prefer your company, with you I do not have to be on my guard. It is going to be difficult for me, especially when we return to Rome, the danger lies in many senior soldiers or politicians. You will see what I mean when we reach Rome."

They went to bed, each concerned with his own thoughts and worries, although Hugh kept an eye on the General as he had almost drunk a whole jar of ouzo by himself. The next morning Hugh woke as someone was pacing to and fro overhead, so as the sun was just beginning to show itself above the eastern sea, sparkling on the water, he decided to go and investigate. Not surprisingly the General was still asleep. When he arrived on deck it was to find the Captain pacing to and fro. When he enquired he was told by the Captain that he was waiting for some fresh vegetables that he had been told would be delivered first thing this morning. Hugh said, "I appreciate your concern Captain, but you are walking overhead of the General, who had plenty to drink yesterday evening, so I would not wake him up by walking to and fro unless you wish him to be annoyed."

"Oh yes," commented the Captain, "I did not realise what I was doing! I am sorry if I disturbed you."

"Will we be staying here very long?" asked Hugh deliberately changing the subject.

"Possibly half a day, but then we must take the vegetables to Rome, or they will not be fresh. So you have plenty of time. What did you want to go and see?"

"I was fascinated by those animals on the rock, is there any way of going to watch them more closely?"

"Yes there is, if you go and ask in the tavern you will be told where to find a guide. Although it is quite a difficult climb, but I don't think that will be a problem for you."

Hugh went to find the guide and found him by just asking a couple of people who pointed him out. The man was actually selling one of the baby apes. He told Hugh, "They make good pets, as long as you look after them and allow them to climb around your home." He was very happy to show Hugh how to reach the apes, that were quite friendly, particularly when they were tempted by a fruit that was completely new to Hugh. It was called a banana and the guide told Hugh that it came from Africa. The guide gave a banana to Hugh as a gift because the yellow fruits fascinated Hugh. He now realised what the cargo must have been; these yellow fruits had originally been green, grew in large bunches and were possibly the main reason why the Captain was now keen to move on towards their final destination. Hugh thanked the guide and then hurried back to the galley, which was now ready to leave the docks and sail east, maybe stopping briefly in Corsica before going on to Naples, the nearest port to Rome. Hugh had studied the charts in the captain's cabin when the General, who had showed him the way they would go, advising him that they would have to go and meet the Emperor, before they could go on to see the General's sister and of course, Rosanna. He knew that there would be a special ceremony in Rome, when the General was to be presented to Nero himself. He had heard a lot about the Emperor, a lot of which had been derogatory. He realised that he would actually be able to judge himself, then realised with horrible fascination that Senator Latitch would probably be with the Emperor and many of the advisors.

As the galley cleared the port of Gibraltar and raised its sail to catch the light wind blowing from the west. Hugh had the strange feeling that this was all part of his destiny, like meeting his wife, Rosanna and the general, who he had come to think of as a father figure. After all he could not remember his own father and all his early life now seemed to be only vague memory. He was about to go below deck when the Captain and a couple of his crew came to talk to him. "We were wondering if you would be good enough to teach us how to use a sword and shield properly?" The Captain then went on to explain, "You see Tribune we are only a trading galley, but there have been a lot of problems with pirates from some of the Greek islands, so we were wondering if you would be good enough to teach us how to fight against pirates."

Hugh thought a minute, before saying, "To be honest Captain, I know very little of fighting on board ships, but I will certainly help teach your men how to use the sword and shield, although now it is fairly late in the day and I would like some time to think of the best way to teach the sailors. Will it be alright if I start the training tomorrow?"

"Certainly Tribune, I will have the men ready for you in the morning," replied the Captain. Hugh went below deck thinking about how he would go about training the sailors to fight the pirates. He thought that he would like to ask the General if he knew anything about battles at sea, as Hugh believed that they were very different to land battles. When he reached the cabin and went inside he was pleased to see that the General was dressed and not suffering from the previous day's drinking, but was reading one of his scrolls. "I am very pleased to see that you are fine, after all the ouzo that you managed to consume yesterday, it seemed to have quite an unusual taste that ouzo, how is it made?" he asked.

"To be honest, I am not really sure, but I believe that somehow it is distilled from the leftovers of the olives, after they have been pressed to extract the oil, which has many uses. I believe that it is boiled in water with the olive skins, although I am no expert. It is more of a spirit that Greeks drink; as you saw yesterday it is quite clear and you mix it with water, then it goes a milky white but it is a pleasant drink, do you not agree?" the General asked.

"Certainly, what is more obvious, it does not seem to leave you with a sore head in the morning after a long session."

"No Hugh, it just makes you very thirsty. I had to drink a lot of water this morning when I woke up," commented the General.

"That is worth remembering Sir! The English main drink is mead, but that leaves you with a really bad headache if you drink too much, just like the wine that you Romans produce," he grinned apologetically.

"Very true my boy," was the General's response.

"However, I am sure that you came to ask me something?"

"Yes sir, I came to ask how to show the sailors how to fight. I would have no difficulties in showing them how to fight normally with a sword and a shield, but I believe that battles at sea are very different, is that not right?"

"It is most certainly so, Hugh. Sea battles are normally fought with catapults that throw burning balls of fire, before they ram opposing ships. The fighting between the crews is secondary, but you will be very good as an instructor." The General was silent, while he considered, before suggesting, "If you are keen on the idea I think that you will have to teach them how to use long handle pikes."

Hugh thought for a moment before saying, "Yes, I believe that we should include pike training, as well as sword and shield. I will speak to the Captain about it tomorrow." They went to bed after discussing the scroll the General had been reading before.

Hugh went on deck the very next morning, summoning those of the crew who had volunteered to train under his direction. He showed them the basic sword movements, how to parry an enemy attack, as well as the twelve principal movements. He took them through the basic movements and then told them that they should practise by themselves. He then asked them to divide into pairs and try to disarm the opponent; this was very sensible as there was a lot of very poor sword work going on. He moved amongst the sailors and corrected their mistakes, and then he asked the captain who had been watching, how best to keep the enemy away from an attack.

"The best way is to stop them boarding us, so we need to fight them off with pikes."

"That is what the General suggested, have you got any pikes on board?"

"I think we have, although they are very old and possibly rusty, I will go and search for them." He came back a few moments later, carrying some pikes. "I think that these will help us to fight the attackers."

Hugh went below deck and was very pleased to see that the General had already prepared something for him to eat. While he talked, between mouthfuls of bread and fruit, he told the General about the training that he had done that day.

After he had eaten, Hugh went on deck and found the pikes in an untidy heap. He told one of the sailors who had shown an aptitude for using the pike that they needed to be cleaned and sharpened, as well as being placed in a convenient rack that one of the carpenters volunteered to build. It was then becoming late and the sun was sinking in the west, so Hugh told them that the fighting training would continue the next day. He was just wandering back to the cabin that he shared with the General when he noticed one of the slaves who had been watching the sword practice and looked quite fit for a slave. Hugh took a look at the slave's number and told him that if he was interested in joining them, he would have a talk with the Captain and ask if the man could be unchained, but also took his number, which was 97. Hugh spoke to the Captain that evening and they soon agreed that slave 97 could be released, although Hugh wanted to know how he came to be aboard the galley. The Captain said, "let me check in the records." He looked up the slaves number, only to realise that he had served on three other galleys, but had previously been a gladiator, who had supported some people who had disagreed with the emperor, so had been sent to work in the galleys. Hugh thought that slave 97 would be a worthwhile addition to his small defence team, which was agreed to by the Captain. The very next day Hugh continued the training and found that slave 97 was very good now that he was free of the manacles around his legs. They had sores, which the ship's doctor had eased with an ointment, which although this smelled very nasty, certainly seemed to help. Generally the standard of the ships fighting became better and better, then Hugh showed them how to use the pikes to cut any boarding lines that had been thrown on board, as well as to repel any boarders. Hugh then paired off with the slave Thalius, who had been number 97 and found that he was very good and had obviously been a good gladiator. He fought Hugh well although Hugh quite easily got under his guard. Hugh made the point of not using the sword to slash so much, but to thrust at various vital parts of the body, which he marked on a life-size dummy telling the sailors that, "You should always go for a quick kill with a thrust of the sword using the point not a slash like a harvester reaping corn." Hugh was very pleased at how the crew continued their progress and was fairly confident that they could cope with an attack, provided that they were not rammed by an enemy, which would cause the galley to sink.

Therefore he had a chat with the bosun, who was in charge of steering the ship and made sure that they would always try not to be rammed, but that if the galley was attacked they should take avoiding action, although not to worry about being boarded. The General had been watching the training and was very impressed. Afterwards he praised Hugh on his training and said, "Hopefully I will be given charge of possibly two or three legions, so I would like you to be considered a trainer of all my warriors." This was indeed a very high praise from the General, who did not often commend his staff.

As the galley sailed eastwards towards Rome, Hugh could see the outline of a large island just to the northeast of where they were. He asked the Captain exactly where they were and what was the name of that large island, even though they had passed some small islands shortly after leaving Gibraltar. The Captain said, "That is the island that they call Capri, where we may stop. Although I am keen to go on to Rome as quickly as possible, but we may call in at Vivara as we can always re-supply with tomatoes and other vegetables." Towards the evening on that day the wind died down, so the Captain decided to take his Galley into Port Vivara. They only spent one evening there, but it was an opportunity to walk on dry land again, much to the crew's pleasure. Hugh went ashore with Thalius, whom he had come to respect. So he spoke about being a gladiator himself, before he joined the army and he began to know the general.

Thalius asked, "I understand that you were with General Priam when he was in charge of the 9th Legion in Britain and you were the only survivors of the brutal attack of the evil Queen Boadicea, am I correct?"

"Yes Thalius that is so, it seems that everybody knows about it and we will receive a special welcome when we arrive in Rome."

"I think that your welcome will be before you reach Rome, as Rome is not on the coast and the nearest is Naples, so you should expect a welcome there. In fact I would not be surprised if the Emperor himself does come himself, you see everybody knows about the lost Legion and that General Priam was the sole survivor due to the work of one of his Centurions, who was then promoted to be a Tribune."

Hugh could think of no immediate answer, so simply shrugged and made his way back to the Galley.

When Hugh and Thalius returned to the galley they found that everybody was on board awaiting their return. Hugh mumbled an apology to the captain for keeping him waiting. "Do not apologise tribune, you are not really late, as we have only just finished loading the cargo that I will take directly to Naples; it is all fresh food so we must hurry. I certainly hope that we meet no disturbances on the way, because there have been reports of pirates in this area. Yet I now feel reassured by having your small fighting force on the galley." Once again Hugh was at a loss, so simply smiled, and then went bellow deck to find that the general had divided their cabin with a curtain, explaining that he felt that Hugh could share his part of their cabin with the newly reinstated Gladiator Thalius, mentioning that it would possibly save difficult questioning later.

"I understand sir," replied Hugh. He then noticed that an additional slave sleeping mat had been added to their part of the cabin, before organising his and Thalius's sleeping arrangements. The next morning an urgent hammering on the cabin door woke them up. Hugh jumped from his sleeping mat and opened the door to see the frightened face of one of the sailors who stammered an apology. "We're under attack from a small fleet of pirates!" Before they even thought about it, Hugh just beat Thalius to the door.

First Hugh and Thalius had snatched up their swords, and went round quickly on deck. Hugh noticed that the ships that were attacking the galley were not large, but were around the galley and none of them had ramming horns on their bows. Hugh was grateful for this and allowed one of the pirate ships to come along side. At the same time he signalled for his small fighting force to stand ready with the pikes. Almost immediately grappling lines were thrown aboard the galley and the nearest pirate ship came along side. Hugh signalled the sailors, who were ready with the pikes and managed to cut some of the lines, as well as fighting back some of the pirates, who seemed most surprised at this armed resistance, as they had been informed that this was simply a trading galley that was only carrying goods to Naples.

Hugh and Thalius were amongst the fierce resistance and slew many of the pirates who tried to climb aboard. Realising that the pirates were not being allowed to have their own way, with what they had been informed was an ordinary cargo galley, they were ordered by the pirate chief to disengage. But Hugh noticed the pirate chief, a wicked looking ruffian and realised that this manoeuvre was planned and that the pirate chief probably knew who had ordered the attack. Hugh knew that if he could capture the pirate chief, he may well be able to force the truth out of him. Therefore, before the ships parted, he leapt onto the pirates' ship and fought two of the pirates who, amazed at being confronted by such an excellent swordsman, backed away, exposing the pirate chief. He struck the sword from the pirate chief, and with comparative ease grabbed the man by the throat and forced him to near the ship that was still attached to the Roman galley. He threw the pirate chief over the side to land sprawling at Thalius' feet, to whom he shouted, "Hold him there, we shall try and find out more about this attack, as I am sure it was deliberate." Hugh jumped aboard the galley as the remaining wine was released. Hugh noticed that the general had come from below deck and was watching the pirate captains, who were all being held at some point. They were not very well armed and were obviously expecting not to meet any resistance, but had been told that this galley was easy prey. "Who ordered this attack?" demanded Hugh, his face directly in front of the pirate chief. "We were acting on the orders of Senator Latitch," replied the terrified pirate chief.

"You know that the penalty for piracy is beheading?"

"We were told that we simply had to capture and kill General Priam," squealed the terrified pirate. Hugh looked at the General, who had come from his cabin to see what the commotion was all about, Hugh looked across at him and there was a complete understanding between them. "I do not think that his word will have any realistic effect against the Senator," said the general.

"I should imagine that you are perfectly correct sir." Hugh then paused for thought, before replying, "No, I suppose you are right, the words of this wretch will count for nothing, therefore I think that we will carry out the sentence and behead him." Without further ado

Hugh simply chopped the man's head off with an almost contemptuous back swing of his sword. The general went to go below deck, as the rest of the pirates showed no more indication of fighting. In fact all the other pirate ships had turned away. Hugh followed the general below deck where the general sat down on the side of his desk and indicated that Hugh should also be seated, while he spoke. "You see my boy that Senator Latitch probably planned this attack at short notice. Obviously he wants revenge on me, after my sister's threat to mutilate him. We will have to be very careful of Senator Latitch. He is very well connected to the right people and can often delay important decisions or stop various laws that affect his lifestyle."

"I understand General, do you think that Senator Latitch is behind some of the corruption in the government?" The general slid off his desk and walked around Hugh, obviously, deep in thought. "I am wondering if he has anymore surprises for us," said the general. He looked thoughtfully at Hugh and then said, "I do not think that we will have any more problems with pirates, although I would like you to keep your fighting force in training, and as I say, they are doing a very good job." Hugh realised that the discussion was over, so he left the general and returned on deck where all was quiet and it was now becoming late in the evening. He was just thinking about going below deck when the captain came over, but before the captain could speak, Hugh broke the silence, "How much longer will it take us to reach Naples?"

"It should only take about three days. Provided that this wind keeps blowing, we should then sight mount Vesuvius."

"I did not think that there were any mountains by the coast in Italy."

The captain laughed and then asked Hugh, "Do you not have any volcanoes in England?"

"Not that I know of, but I do not really know what a volcano is."

"To be honest, I really am not the person to answer your question, as I am not really sure myself." He then considered before speaking again, "I believe that deep in the earth there is some very hot rock, which occasionally bursts out of the mountains, these mountains are called volcanoes and Mount Vesuvius is an active volcano. It destroyed the town of Pompeii, from where I come, and it still occasionally threatens to erupt again. You will be able to see some smoke rising from the mountain before we see it." Hugh decided to return below deck, wondering about volcanoes as he went.

The next day Hugh spent training his fighting force and had just stopped for lunch, when Thalius came over to speak to him. "I have brought you something to eat Hugh."

"Thank you Thalius, I was beginning to feel hungry." As Hugh had spent a long time thinking about volcanoes, he decided to ask Thalius what he knew about Mount Vesuvius. "Is Mount Vesuvius the only volcano in Italy, or are there any others that you know of?"

"No Hugh, I believe that this is the only one in Italy, but I believe that there is at least one in Sicily, which is a large island to the south off where we are now." It was as if he had guessed Hugh's next question. "The captain told me about Mount Vesuvius," said Hugh, "so I wondered whether you knew anything about it, because it sounds very interesting. You see we do not have any volcanoes in Britain, or not that I am aware of. I was wondering if we would have the opportunity to climb up to the top?"

"We may do, but I think that it will depend on the General, because he has many demands on his time and he may expect us to be with him." As Hugh looked disappointed, Thalius continued speaking, "Yet we may have a chance, although I believe it may be dangerous, because the ground around the mountain shakes, or so I have been told." They ate the remainder of the food Thalius had brought, each preoccupied with his own thoughts. Thalius then broke the silence. "We may have an opportunity if the Emperor plans a special meeting. Maybe we can disappear for a couple of days, but I think that the General ought to be advised if we do go. But what do you think about the idea, and will you ask the General?"

Hugh thought for a moment before replying, "Yes Thalius leave it to me, I will let you know as soon as I know!" Then much to Thalius' surprise, Hugh pointed to the east, "Could that smoke be coming from the mountain?"

Thalius looked in the direction that Hugh was pointing and said, "I think you may be correct, therefore we may reach there tomorrow."

That evening Hugh made a special point of talking to General Priam. "When we arrive in Naples sir, do you think it would be possible for me and Centurion Thalius to try to climb Mount Vesuvius?

The General chewed thoughtfully on his food before replying, "I would like to say yes Hugh, although it really depends upon what I may have to do. I cannot really grant you permission at the moment, although I will bear your request in mind.

"Thank you sir, for I appreciate your difficulty and we will just hope that it all will be possible."

"In fact Hugh I would be very interested to come with you myself, but I do not think it will be possible. You see the last time I was in Naples it was about eight years ago and I went halfway up myself with a friend and it was very unusual. The ground often shakes, although the local people do not consider there is anything to worry about. Many people have foretold that it is a warning from the Gods who do not like many of the things that go on in places like Pompeii. This is where Senator Latitch holds many of his extravagant parties, like the one that he wanted to take your wife to, before he knew that you and I were still alive. Well you remember the rest of the story! Therefore Hugh what I am saying is that you ought to be on your guard, because Senator Latitch is a man who does not like being beaten. Now you have twice thwarted him so be very careful. Do I make myself clear?"

"Yes, you most certainly do sir."

The following day they arrived in Naples Harbour, where there was a special reception committee who had come from Rome especially to meet the General, who was treated like an honoured guest. Obviously a lot of the glory was reflected onto Hugh and he spotted his enemy amongst the well-wishers and he felt sure that he caught Senator Latitch glancing at him and whispering to one of his large bodyguards who gave an evil grin in reply.

The following morning, when Hugh was just having a wash after his normal workout, he was approached by the same bodyguard who Senator Latitch had spoken to and he was surprised to learn that the General's party would not be leaving for Rome immediately. "We were told by the general that you and one of your centurions were very interested in seeing some of the sights up on the mountain, I will be delighted to show you some of the sights, particularly as I am on a day's leave and intending to take a few others with me, so I would be very happy to have you join the group."

Hugh responded immediately and made arrangements to meet the man with Centurion Thalius, although the General's warning was increased when the man told them that he had already passed on a message to the General. Centurion Thalius came up to Hugh and told him that their wish had come true. "It was rather strange, because I was told that we would need no extra provisions."

"Just guess, that is virtually what I was told, although I think that we should take quarter staffs with us, presumably you know how to use a quarter staff. If anyone asks tell them that it was my idea." So they set out together with sturdy ash quarter staffs.

They met the guide who had offered to show them the way and noticed that he was accompanied by four other large beefy men, built along the same lines as nearly all the senator's bodyguards, with plenty of muscle, but very few brains. Almost at once one of the large men asked, "What did you bring the sticks for?"

"We always use these quarter staffs when we are going for a walk in the hills, so we thought that it would be a good idea," said Hugh.

"Just more to carry," snarled one of the others.

"We could ask why you are all armed," enquired Thalius.

"Obviously we are both soldiers, so it is normal for us to carry weapons. But you are civilians, so what is your excuse?" The man who was the guide swiftly interjected, "We will take you through the new palace which is being built a little further to the north east, this is an extension of Pompeii and the new temple has many interesting decorations, that not every person has seen and in fact you are very lucky that I am around to show you."

"Lead on," invited Hugh, and he noticed that three of the large men hung back, so that Hugh and Thalius were sandwiched between the large men. Hugh pointed this out and in an undertone to Thalius he mentioned, "We must keep our wits about us, because I am sure that this has all been carefully planned."

"I am sure that you are right," whispered Thalius. After a short while some of the large men felt that the pace of the tribune and his centurion was too difficult for them to easily keep up, as they did not expect soldiers who had been on a long voyage to be so fit. Their guide had also realised this and thought that he would try to spring his trap earlier than he had originally intended, so he said, "We go in here," pointing to a new archway. When they were halfway through the arch the leader tried to spring his trap, but he did not realise that Hugh was right behind him and Thalius was on the right, but he was left-handed so used his quarter staff in the other hand. One of the following large men went to draw his sword, which was instantly knocked from his hand with a sharp blow on his wrist, delivered by Hugh, and as their guide turned round with his sword in his hand he received a savage bash from Thalius across his face. Realising that it had all gone terribly wrong, the large men all fled in terror from Hugh and Thalius who chuckled at their easy victory. When they had finished laughing, Hugh said, "Have you seen the pictures on this archway? I am sure that they hoped that we would be intrigued by the erotic paintings."

"It does not really interest me," said Thalius almost indifferently. "Needless to say they hoped that we would be more interested and not expect their attack, but now we have the rest of the day to explore the mountain."

The rest of that day was spent climbing up to the top of the mountain, which was considerably difficult, due mainly to the atmosphere. Just before they reached the top Hugh said, "It smells worse than an unwashed latrine."

"Yes, a grey area."

"Actually it smells as if they all ate rotten eggs!" Eventually the ground made a very violent tremble just when they reached the crater and they could peer down through the smoke and see hot bubbling liquid rock, from which the smell was coming.

"Well we finally made it," said Hugh, "but I suggest that we make a hasty tactical withdrawal, before we are tipped into the awful morass, or choked to death." And they hastily retreated down hill and they were glad that they had brought quarter staffs which they used to steady themselves scrambling down the sides of the volcano, on their way back to Pompeii.

When they met General Priam that evening before dinner, Hugh told him about the fracas with Senator Latitch's bodyguards, at which the General guffawed as he told them that they had done very well. He was then handed a scroll from a messenger, which he looked at breaking the heavy wax seal, which had an unmistakable cartouche, proclaiming that it was from one of the Senator's Enrobe. He scowled as he read and said to Hugh, "I will reply to this and send a copy to the Emperor, as it is an unofficial complaint about one of my tribunes and one of his accompanying centurions, who made an unprovoked attack on the senator's bodyguards, when they were simply acting as guides. So I will make a reply, with a copy to the Emperor, telling him exactly what you told me. Unfortunately the Emperor is rather weak at carrying out the orders of his senate, even though they may be crazy. It is regrettable, but that is the sad situation at the moment. Needless to say, you will probably meet the Emperor when we arrive in Rome; that way you will be able to judge for yourselves. We shall be leaving for Rome tomorrow morning. It is normally just a full days march, but as we seem to have to travel like a bloody circus, it will take at least two days before we arrive and I really have no idea of how long we will be before I can give you leave to visit Rosanna, who as you know is staying with my sister in Pisa. Obviously you will wish to see your wife and of course your son, who is apparently a fine boy, just like his father." It was true that Hugh wanted to see his wife and son, but he was used to the army by now and knew that he would have to comply with army regulations, particularly if the general was given the command of one or more legions, as he had predicted would be the case.

General Priam was quite correct and they had to travel in procession. The general was riding on a new horse that was a gift from the commander in Naples, while Hugh was in a chariot accompanied by Thalius, who took the reins. They travelled at just over a marching pace and the road was lined with cheering crowds, who were simply ordered out, although they did not really know what they were cheering about. It seemed to be a standard thing, because Naples was the normal port for Roman galleys and the crowd were normally cheering a further addition to the Roman Empire, even though many additions were still problem areas. This reminded Hugh of the general's writings about how a country needed to be properly subjugated. It made Hugh wonder about the uprising in Britain and whether all of the tribes had really started to develop Roman ways. He very much doubted it; this seemed to be a case of whether or not the people believed in the justice of Roman rule and whether or not they agreed with the gods of Rome. Now the Emperor was a supposed god and if Nero was crazy, as the General had suggested, then they were fighting a losing battle. The cheering crowds began to irritate Hugh after a while, his mind began to think about how he would organise a marching legion, so some of the soldiers exercised more than just their legs, even though the average soldier had to carry all his equipment, which was a considerable amount. They stopped for lunch only after the cheering crowds had dispersed and they ate dates and olives with a type of biscuit.

They stopped in a village, where accommodation was provided and Hugh was sharing a room with Thalius, next to the general's suite. In the room the walls were very thin and it was very easy to hear everything that was being said, so Hugh pointed this out to Thalius, "Do you think that this is deliberate?"

"I am sure that it is, so we must be very careful of what we say, as I am sure that there is someone who will listen to everything." After a while Thalius produced some dice, so they spent the evening playing dice not for money, but for small lengths of straw.

The next day was fairly similar; although they did not have many crowds to cheer them, so they made better progress towards Rome, although they only reached the outskirts of that great city, supposedly the greatest city in the world, where they stayed the night. This was because General Priam wanted to enter the city in the morning and make a spectacular entrance into the Coliseum. Hugh had often wondered what Rome was like, but nothing had prepared him for his first sight of such a city. It made Londonium seem like a village. He asked Thalius, who did not seem to be so impressed, "I did not imagine a city so large, it will take a day to walk from one side to the other."

"I never thought that I would see it again," exclaimed Thalius. "I was actually born here, but it does not feel like home at all. I cannot even remember where we used to live."

"I can well believe that," said Hugh. "When we were in Britain, I did not feel at home although it is really nearly the only thing I remember. What did give me a feeling of belonging was when we passed near to the village from where I used to go out to sea in my fishing boat." He then went on to explain about how he met General Priam, who showed him to Aurolius who had trained him as a gladiator. "Well I'm sure that I have told you the rest of my story, but who did you offend?"

"Well it's quite a long story, although you may not be surprised because it was Senator Latitch!"

Hugh thought about this and realised that there must be a lot of people whom the evil senator had affected. He stood in thought for quite a long time and wondered about the political situation and realised that it may well depend on having a strong emperor, and with a sharp realisation he realised that he would meet Emperor Nero the following day. He turned away and followed Thalius back to the room they were sharing. After a while Hugh asked Thalius, "Did you have any women when you were a gladiator?"

"Yes Hugh," Thalius replied, "but there was one special friend, of whom it could be said was my undoing." He looked thoughtful and because of that Hugh did not interrupt him, as he was sure that he would continue with the story. "Yes, her name was Titonia and she was very lovely, with golden hair and enchanting blue eyes, just like sapphires. The strange thing was that she was not really to blame, as you can well imagine, she was very noticeable. It was Senator Latitch who took her from me to use her as one of the serving girls at one of his parties. So I never saw her again!" Hugh was about to offer some words of comfort, when General Priam walked in through the door. He looked at Hugh and said, "When we arrive in the Coliseum tomorrow morning I will want you to drive my chariot, when we will be taken to the emperor, who has asked me to introduce you to him. At least that is what the message that I have just received tells me. Although it comes from Nero, I doubt whether he wrote it or even really knows, but you will meet him tomorrow, so I will let you judge for yourself." He then paused, as if collecting his thoughts. "I am going to ask for some leave to visit my sister and our family's estate in Pisa, and of course to take you with me. I have no doubt that you will want to see your Rosanna and your son!"

"Most certainly sir," was all that Hugh could say. It was as if all Hugh's wishes had come true, and he could not quite believe it.

* * * * *

Cynthia Priam was reading aloud, from a letter that she had just received from her brother. It said: 'I am back in Rome with Hugh and shall be presented tomorrow to the Emperor, who I expect will give me a new command. However I will ask for some leave so that I can return to Pisa to see you and sort out any pressing problems with the estate, although I am very confident that you have everything under control. Obviously I will hope to bring Hugh with me, as he will want to see Rosanna and his son. Hopefully the Emperor will grant my wish, but cannot be definite. W we will meet fairly soon, although I do not know for certain or for how long it will be'. He then put his cartouche on the base of the letter. She looked up at Rosanna who was holding her baby and was smiling.

"Did you hear that Petros, daddy will soon be with us, isn't that good news?" The baby grinned and gurgled as she juggled him in her arms.

"Well that sounds very promising, let's hope that the emperor grants him plenty of time to spend with us, before he is sent away again," said Cynthia to Rosanna, and some of the other girls who were listening.

"Your brother, the General, was the only survivor with Hugh, from the 9th Legion after the uprising in Britain?" asked Lydia.

"Yes my dear, I am afraid so," said Cynthia kindly. "I realise that this confirms that you are a widow, because Hugh and my brother were the only survivors. However you must not lose hope, you are still young and attractive, I'm sure that you will have no difficulty in finding a new husband," said Cynthia, whose words were met with a murmur of agreement from many of the other girls who were all soldiers' wives. It was fairly common for a young woman to have been married to two or possibly three soldiers. Like most armies, the roman legions were for ordinary men and there was always a plentiful supply of women wherever they were garrisoned. In many cases soldiers did not care very much for their woman, in fact not all the women in Cynthia Priam's villa were certain that their born even belonged to the men that they had married. This was a very common situation and this was one of the reasons that made Rosanna feel special, not only did she feel very much for Hugh, but she was totally devoted to the baby as well as Hugh.

Life returned to normal in Cynthia Priam's villa, even though there was an air of expectancy. The situation was relieved when three horsemen rod up to the gates of the villa They were the general, Hugh and Thalius. When they dismounted and gave the reins of the horses to the grooms and walked into the villa they were met with a cry of relief and joy from both Cynthia and Rosanna, plus a lot of cries of welcome to all three men. "There was no time to warn you of our coming, as we came straight from the Coliseum where we were met by the emperor who has given me and my tribune at least twenty days leave, but I will then have to take my leave of you again, because I now have three legions under my command," announced the general proudly. Rosanna had rushed over to Hugh as soon as she saw him, while she had almost flung young Petros at Lydia, who stood fairly awkwardly watching the reunion between Rosanna and Hugh. This was very emotional, as was the meeting of the General with Cynthia. Thalius felt almost excluded and he looked across at Lydia and their eyes met. There was an immediate liking between them, not only because their best friends had fallen into a deep embrace, but there was also a mutual attraction. After a while Cynthia Priam released the general and became more like her old self, taking charge over everybody. Even Hugh and Thalius found it quite unusual to see the general being bossed about, even though Cynthia was a lot smaller and a couple of years younger than her brother. The men were allocated to their rooms, although Hugh was allowed to share with Rosanna and the baby, whom he was delighted to take from Lydia. As Rosanna had previously been sharing with Lydia, it made Lydia have to move to another room, although she made certain that Thalius knew where she was sleeping, and although Hugh was feeling preoccupied with Rosanna and Petros, he noticed the exchange between Thalius and Lydia.

The stay in Pisa was very enjoyable, but like most holidays seemed to be too brief and before they had really settled down it was time for them to depart, much to the dismay of Hugh and also Thalius and Lydia, who were making no secret of their liking for one another and were sleeping together. The horses had been brought around to the front of the villa, where they had also enjoyed the easy time and where they had been well cared for, carefully groomed and well fed, far better than if they had been stabled in their normal army stables. As the general mounted his horse he said to Cynthia, "I have to return and organise my new legions, even though I do not yet know where we will be sent, but I will let you know as soon as may be." Here he paused for a while and then said, "Maybe I can and possibly even try to visit you again." He then gave Hugh and Thalius a knowing wink, before turning his horse onto the road and trotting off with Hugh and Thalius following reluctantly.

Part Three

"Jews and Christians"

The new barracks were situated in the northeast of the great city of Rome, they were well laid out and nearly all the equipment was new, from sword and shield to chariots and horses. Hugh was very pleased to have Thalius as one of his centurions, but was well aware that he should not show any particular favouritism under his direct supervision. Like most senior officers in the army he had quite the share of paper work. That kept him very busy most evenings, although he did manage to make a few forays into Rome, mainly to Taverns where many of his fellow soldiers were to be found. Although he was very friendly with many, he basically kept to himself and made sure that he never drank too much, or became involved in gambling or carousing like so many soldiers. He saw General Priam quite often and he was aware that the general was often mindful of not showing any particular favouritism to him. His duties kept him so occupied that it was quite a shock to realise that almost fifty days had passed since they had taken the new soldiers, who were mainly youngsters but who were very keen and competitive. They all knew of his reputation and were always trying to impress him with their skills, although he was extremely diligent in keeping his body in shape and was often seen doing exercises, quite unlike many of his fellow senior officers. It became a standing joke that he was trying to become the youngest Legatus in the army.

He was not really surprised when he received a letter from Rosanna, telling him that Lydia was expecting. He read on with a smile and knew that Centurion Thalius would be calling in to tell him that he was going to be a father. Sure enough some time later there was a knock on the door and in response to his saying "Enter," Thalius was revealed looking quite embarrassed! "I am sorry to bother you sir, but I was wondering if I may take some leave?"

Hugh tried to look stern, although after a very short while he could not contain his smile and he went on to say, "Of course you can have four or five days, which is customary, now I will possibly try to come with you, if the general agrees. I will take any advantage that I can to see my own wife and son again. So we have plenty to celebrate, I will join you for a drink this evening after training has finished." He then walked round his desk and clapped his friend on the back, "You old rascal Thalius. I suppose you will marry the girl now, which is the right thing to do." He dismissed Thalius and went to see the general, who was not surprised to see him, after Hugh had closed the door, to give them some privacy.

"I know what you want to ask, you see I received a scroll from my sister this morning." Here he pointed to one of the scrolls on his desk and then continued, "I know that you wish to take a few days leave as well as Thalius, so I will grant that for you provided that you do not allow Thalius to become too intoxicated tonight, because we will have to be careful tomorrow, as we are due to escort some of the senators to the Coliseum tomorrow and of course the hangmen's dilemma will be one of the bastards!" He grinned as he dismissed Hugh, to whom he gave a knowing wink. That evening after duty, Hugh met Thalius in the mess from where they would go to the Taverna for a celebratory drink. On the way he told Thalius what the general had advised, which had the effect of wiping the grin from Thalius' face.

"Are you serious Hugh," he asked?

"I am my friend, therefore we have to be careful," Hugh replied.

Hugh was very impressed with the guard for the senators, when he inspected them in the morning, because he knew that any minor defect would be noticed. He had taken particular care when he had dressed that morning, wanting to ensure that no report would be made about the guard. Taking his place at the front of the guards he marched them smartly to the gateway of the Senate, were he announced their presence to the officer on duty. He made sure that they lined up into ranks with a space for the senators in-between. The men had been drilled into marching a reasonably slow pace that they would adjust to pace of the senators' walk, which was a lot slower than the normal marching pace. The senators came out and positioned themselves between the columns of soldiers, and wandered off, as if they were just out for a stroll, casually chatting to each other about nothing in particular. The hangmen's dilemma was there and seeing Hugh made a loud derogatory remark about the General and Hugh, but without his customary bodyguards he looked even more feeble and vulnerable than usual. The guard duty was mainly because it made the senators feel important, but also it was necessary, because the senators were liable to be attacked by any of the Roman citizens, due to their unpopularity. Hugh knew that this display of casual elegance was just an act, based on the Greeks, whom they had tried to mimic, but the state of democracy in Rome was quite farcical.

They were almost at the Coliseum, when Hugh suddenly realised what was happening. To his left was a chariot that appeared to be out of control, without a charioteer or passenger, but the horses were obviously out of control and were heading directly for the group of senators. Without even thinking about what he was doing Hugh grabbed a spear from the nearest soldier and held it levelled at the horse's chest, with the butt of the spear firmly wedged into the hard earth, as he knew that no horse would charge directly onto a spear, if it could avoid such a suicidal death. The spear was aimed at the horse on the left and Hugh planned to sever the horse's tendons if it swerved away into the line of the other horse. Whatever had caused the horse to bolt, did not completely madden it and it careered into the other horse, just as Hugh had intended. The effect of this was to entangle the horses and the chariot crashed onto its side, where it skidded to a halt just in front of Hugh. A small child was hurled from the chariot and Hugh ordered one of his centurions to look after the boy, while he went to calm the horses. The one who had seemingly gone berserk, was still jittering in its traces although its companion stood quite calmly, even though it was snorting after the exertion of its wild charge. As Hugh patted the calm horse he could feel the heat of the other crazy horse and realised that it needed bleeding, so he withdrew his dagger and opened one of the pulsating veins in the horse's neck, twisting the point of his dagger, to allow a bright jet of hot blood to spurt from the wound. After counting to ten he withdrew his dagger and the wound closed, while he did this the horse stood calmly. Hugh resheathed his dagger after wiping the blade on the horse's harness and spitting on the small wound he had inflicted, effectively sealing the cut by wiping his thumb over the wound.

A man came running after the runaway chariot, shouting out, "By the gods I am sorry, the grey horse just went wild and I could not hold him, but is my son alright?"

Hugh replied, "I think so sir, he's been looked after by one of my soldiers, but I am afraid your chariot is probably beyond repair."

"As long as nobody was hurt, that is the main thing," said the owner of the chariot.

"You should take his name and chain him up," demanded Senator Latitch. "I would also be grateful if somebody could shut that bloody child up, there is nothing worse than a bawling kid!"

"I think you are being very unfair Latitch," said one of the other senators.

"I mean if it had not been for the bravery of the Tribune, some of us would have been ridden down. I think you are acting very unreasonably!" Hugh thought that he recognised the senator who had just spoken, or at least there was something familiar about his face.

"Alright, alright we'll leave it, but let's move on and take our places, or the entertainment will start without us, you know that the emperor is attending and the fool will probably start without waiting for us."

When they arrived in the Coliseum, Hugh ushered the senators to their seats and stood at the back of their box. They were indeed just in time as the bugles rang out and all the spectators in the Coliseum listened to the afternoon's events that were shouted to the crowd by an orator. It seemed that there was going to be some punishments first.

Hugh could hear Senator Latitch calling out to his fellow senators, that he really enjoyed this, because all the people who did not strictly follow Roman law should be put to death and this was good entertainment as well. It seemed that the people who were being brought out into the arena were a group of people from a Roman province called Judea and they were led out under guard, but the guards then retreated behind large wooden shields. It then became clear why some bars were lifted from an enclosure, which Hugh could not see. The group of people in the arena simply huddled together, as several large sandy coloured cats bounded into the arena snarling and spitting. Hugh had seen wild cats in Britain, but nothing as large as these, they were almost as large as ponies and looked very formidable. Hugh remembered that his old friend Adobe had told him about these animals, but Adobe had told him that although they were very vicious, they normally would not hunt humans, although it was considered to be a mark of manhood to kill one of them with a spear. Apparently, they normally hunted other wild animals and it was mainly the females who did the hunting. They were noticeable because they did not have a large a shaggy mane of hair. The prisoners who were huddled together were all terrified and a couple ran from the lions, trying to reach the safety of the large shields. Their bid for safety was futile, as the Roman soldiers kept them away from the shields at spear point and the cats pounced on them from behind, tearing their backs with vicious claws, as well as sinking their fangs and tearing mouthfuls of flesh. Hugh felt that this was totally unnecessary and quite repugnant, although many of the crowd seemed to enjoy the show, laughing and calling jeers at some of the terrified prisoners particularly when one of them voided his bowels. Many of the senators seemed to enjoy this, in particular Senator Latitch who chuckled with amazing gusto. Hugh was pleased to notice that none of his command was enjoying the spectacle and they remained straight faced, as if carved from stone. About the only senator who did not seem to enjoy this spectacle was the man who Hugh thought he had seen before, so he made a mental note to find out who this senator was. The afternoon wore on, with the other bloodthirsty events, like a couple of prisoners being beheaded, as the orator shouted the events that would be coming over the next few days before the start of the sporting events, which sounded interesting. Hugh was grateful when they ushered the senators away from the coliseum having completed their duty.

When he entered his own office the next morning Hugh was surprised to find that General Priam was waiting for him. "Ah good, I am pleased to see you all in one piece," he laughed, mainly at the quizzical expression on Hugh's face. "I am here to congratulate you on what you did yesterday, even if saving Senator Latitch was not really your intention."

"Well no Sir, I did not have a chance to think, I was simply following orders to leave the party safe," explained Hugh.

"Well it was very well done Hugh, you seem to be able to make unexpected friendships by saving people," he laughed. "You see one of the senators was recently married to my sister, before she decided to throw him out, although he is still quite reasonable, for a senator," these last three words were emphasised. Hugh then knew why he thought he had recognised the senator, because his children were in Pisa at the villa run as an orphanage and training school for soldier's children, where Rosanna was staying. It was as if the pieces of a jigsaw were coming together, he thought he had better let the General continue with what he was obviously going to tell him, so he did nothing but look at the General expectantly.

"Yes Hugh," said General Priam, "I am afraid that we will probably have to leave Rome, although not immediately. "I think I will be able to give you a couple of days leave before we must finish the training and be ready to leave Rome. My sources, which are normally very accurate, suggest that we will be on the move again, this time we will possibly be heading for Judea. Oh yes," he said suddenly remembering what he had originally come to talk about, "the man whose son had been in the runaway chariot, which you stopped, is a very important merchant, a man called Zacceus. Well, he comes from Judea and he was very grateful for what you did, so he may well prove to be a useful contact and it was really because of him that Senator Latitch was unable to make any accusations against you," here he lowered his voice and said, "although he is a Jew, which is the name that is given to the people who come from Judea and the province to the north, which is called Israel or sometimes referred to as Galilei. You see money counts for a lot in Rome. I suppose that it is always the case in any country, whether it is a democracy, or a tyranny." He finished speaking and left, leaving Hugh still slightly confused. Hugh tried to put it to the back of his mind. What had previously been a safe place was safe no longer. Visions of Senator Latitch kept intruding and he was thinking of going out for a run or doing something physical, when there was a knock on the door. "Enter," called out Hugh automatically. One of the guards outside his office put his hand around the door and said, "There is a man to see you Tribune, he is very insistent and says that the general has given him permission to see you, so I dare not send him away, at least not without your authority," he looked at Hugh obviously expecting an answer.

"Alright tell him to wait just a little while and I will call him in, by the way what is his name?"

"Zacceus, Ben Zacceus," came the reply. Hugh realised that this must be the man whose son he had rescued from the chariot, because Zacceus was obviously the man that General Priam had mentioned, so Hugh sat behind his desk and took out a couple of scrolls to look as if he had been engrossed in his work. He recalled that he had read about the Jewish faith, and remembered that they used the name Ben just like the British used son on the end of a name to indicate that person was the son of the name that it preceded. He then went over a piece of doggerel in his mind, which ran, 'one, two, three, four let him wait outside the door', before he called out, "Enter."

The small man he recognised came in and almost threw himself on Hugh, "May the Lord bless you, sir."

Hugh was somewhat embarrassed by this situation, but recovered quickly and said, "There is no need for histrionics, as I was only doing my duty!"

"But my friend, I am in your debt," he shrugged before continuing, "I must reward you," he then took a look around to make sure that they were indeed alone.

Before he could speak again Hugh forestalled him, because things seemed to suddenly take shape in Hugh's confused mind. He realised that this man could be of great value to him. "Zacceus what do you know about Judea?"

"My life, my boy. What do I know about my own land, it will fill a library," he shrugged again.

Hugh had realised that the small man's manner of speaking was characterised with body language and tried to ignore it. He eventually managed to sit Zacceus down and he finally learnt a lot from this unexpected source.

That evening he was telling Thalius all about the strange encounter with Zacceus, who told him all about Judea, and that General Priam was sure that they would be going to Judea soon. "At least it sounds an extraordinary place. The people there have this strange belief in that there is only one god and they simply call him the Lord, yet Priam told me that he is called Yahweh," Hugh exclaimed.

"I think I have heard something about it," said Thalius, "does it not have a capital city called Jerusalem?"

"Yes that is correct, apparently it's a real problem area because they forbid the Roman eagles to come into the temple area, but it sounds to me like its very hypocritical, because they allow all sorts of other things and they are always arguing amongst themselves about what is correct and what is not right. Apparently crucified a man instead of a notorious robber," Hugh sighed.

"Sounds like a real bundle of fun," grimaced his friend. "Priam reckons we will have a few days leave, so have you any idea of when we can go to Pisa?"

"No, but I think he was trying to imply that it will be soon, so just concentrate on that and be thankful," said Hugh.

* * * * *

Rosanna was busy teaching her young ladies needlework, when she heard the sound of horses coming to the villa and the voice of one of the grooms saying, "Yes Sir, I will take good care of the horses, so the centurions and your own horse will be well looked after Tribune." Rosanna realised that this must be Hugh, so with a shout of joy she ran to the door, deserting her young ladies. Rosanna ran to Hugh and flung herself into his arms, she was closely followed by Lydia who embraced Thalius in a more than crushing hug. Eventually the girls left their men to recover their breath and lead them into the villa, where Cynthia Priam met them in a formal fashion, shaking them by the hands and inviting them to drink a goblet of wine. Hugh said, "Thank you Cynthia for your gracious welcome, Thalius and I will only be able to stay for five days, but if there is any work that you would like us to do, please feel free to ask."

"Thank you for your kind offer, but I have everything under control, although I will bear it in mind because I often have some jobs for fit young men like you!"

Later on that same day, after Rosanna had finished her teaching and Thalius was ensconced with Lydia. Rosanna spoke quietly with Hugh when they were close together, "I think I may well be pregnant again, as I have missed my last period and have not been feeling very fit in the morning over the last week, although it is probably to early to be sure, what do you think?"

"Well, I suppose it is possible after all we certainly were very passionate on my last visit." He paused for a while thinking, before saying, "It would be fine for Petros to have a sibling to play with."

"I suppose I am in a fine place, although I have not said anything to Cynthia, yet she would be quite happy," said Rosanna. As it was a nice evening, Hugh and Rosanna went for a walk around the estate through the orchard, where there were some very larges old trees at the boundary. Hugh was carrying Petros and told Rosanna all about his meeting with Zacceus, before telling her General Priam had a feeling he would be sent out to Judea, telling her that it was a trouble spot and some of the problems that the Roman army had encountered. Young Petros was very lively and kept trying to draw Hugh's dagger or sword when he did not keep an eye on what the boy was doing. "He is going to be just like his father," laughed Rosanna.

"He is rather young to start using a weapon, particularly anything sharp. It maybe your responsibility to make sure that he does not injure himself or anyone else," Hugh replied. While they were talking Hugh noticed that one of the large trees had a couple of dead branches that looked as if they could easily break off and injure someone so when they got back to the villa he left Petros to be fed by Rosanna and went to find Cynthia. She was in the kitchens, supervising the cooking of the evening meal. Hugh spoke of the trees at the back of the orchard. She told him that the gardener was away at the moment." Hugh told her that the trees, should really be chopped down and used for firewood. "That is an easy job that Thalius and I could easily do for you, would you like us to arrange it?"

"Yes, if you and Thalius could do it, but make sure that you keep the area clear of children. You know they like to watch people with axes, of which there are a couple in the gardener's work shed. Therefore, I will leave it for you and Thelius to arrange when you will do it."

"I think that tomorrow morning would be a good time, because we normally start the day early and all the children will be having breakfast, but I must check with Thalius first."

Early the next morning Hugh and Thalius selected a couple of large axes from the gardener's tool shed and went to where the old trees stood. They had to be fairly accurate in the way they cut down the trees because the trees were fairly large and could easily knock down young orchard fruit trees when they fell. Thelius said, "Have you ever cut down large trees before? Because I have not and I understand it can be quite a difficult job, so we must be careful. I hate to think what General Priam would do to us if we ruined his orchard."

"Don't worry Thalius I have cut plenty of trees when I was young and built my first boat. What you have to do is to undercut the tree on the side where it will fall and then make the basic chopping down strokes on the other side. It will keep you fit; you thought you were on holiday, but you know me, I like to make sure all my centurions are kept in good shape," Hugh chuckled. He took some chalk from his pouch and marked an area about three fingers width above the ground, he then stood back and made sure that Thalius was at least five paces away. Then, with his legs firmly placed a few cubits apart, he swung the axe that buried itself into the wood directly at the place he had marked. The whole tree gave a shiver and a lot of leaves rained down onto Hugh, who freed the axe with a jerk and delivered a second heavy blow, at which a triangular wedge fell out from the cut that had been made. He went on with his work until the tree was partially severed, then he went around to the other side of the tree and began chopping again, using large sweeping blows that made the wood chips fly about him. Eventually the tree gave a final groan and fell directly as Hugh had planned right between the other trees, but without damaging them. Hugh was now sweating profusely and slipped off his tunic top, so the muscles on his arms and shoulders stood out, making him look incredibly fit. He lent on the axe haft, while Thalius applauded his work.

Hugh said to Thalius, "It's your turn now, you have seen how its done, so you mark the next tree and I will check it before you start wielding the axe." Thalius did just the same as Hugh had previously done and was now sweating profusely and much to his delight the tree lay exactly where they planned for it to fall. There were now a group of larger children from the villa who had come to watch, although Hugh made sure that they kept well away from the swinging axe and the flying wood chips. Hugh cut down the next tree, much to everybody's delight; this time Thalius made sure that Hugh was uninterrupted in his work, this was fairly difficult, as there were now many people who had come to watch, even Cynthia Priam had come to check all this activity. The three felled trees now needed chopping into manageable lengths and then splitting until they could be used as firewood. Once again Hugh and Thalius undertook this work, after a well-earned drink of flavoured water from the fruits in the orchard. Most of the children were not so keen on watching this, although a couple of the older boys were quite fascinated and asked Hugh if they could help, so he gave them small jobs to do, which helped the work go smoothly and by the late afternoon there was a sizable pile of branches and split logs that were carried back to the villa, where Rosanna and Lydia were seen praising their men. Thalius and Hugh were the last to return and Thalius could be heard complaining that he had blisters on his left hand, because he was very much right handed and not as ambidextrous as Hugh, who often changed his grip so that one hand was always stationary although the other hand would slide down the axe haft. "Well it will possibly keep you quiet tonight, as well as giving Lydia a good night's sleep."

"What do you mean Hugh?"

Hugh looked at him and grinned, "Well you were banging away all last night, it's certainly kept Rosanna and I awake, to be honest I am surprised that Cynthia Priam did not tell you off."

Their five days stay was eventually over, much to everybody's regret, even Cynthia Priam told them that their stay was most welcome, as she had found plenty of jobs for them. However, it was Lydia and Rosanna who were the saddest to watch them ride away back to Rome, because they did not think they would see them again before they sailed away to Judea, as Hugh was fairly certain that they would be going there almost as soon as they returned to Rome. He did not realise that he was slightly mistaken and it would be only a short while before they set out for that fascinating land. Their return to the barracks was quite uneventful and they both were feeling depressed, when a messenger found them only half a day's ride from the barracks. He had some very surprising news for them. Hugh took the scroll from the messenger and read it aloud to Thalius. "It seems," said Hugh, "that we must hurry back to the barracks, as there appears to be a minor revolution at Salerno in the south of Italy, so the general requires us to go with one legion, which is all he can spare at the moment. But it should be enough to put down the revolution that is being led by a gladiator from Thrace, who is called Spartacus and he has rallied some of the slaves to form a fighting force."

Thalius looked at Hugh and said, "you know that rings a bell, I feel sure that I have heard the name before, obviously it was a long time ago when I was gladiator myself, but I feel sure that I have met this Spartacus."

"Well let's move and see if we can organise one of the legions to move tomorrow, as it sounds very urgent." Therefore they moved into a gallop from just trotting along, hoping to arrive at the barracks and find that the Legate in charge of one of the legions would have everything in readiness.

When they reached the barracks their horses were tired and sweating profusely, although Hugh was delighted to see that everybody was as busy as ants, rushing around and making sure that everything was in readiness to leave at the break of dawn tomorrow. He also noted that his immediate commander of the legion who was Legatus Marcus Anthony was waiting for them. Hugh threw the reins of his horse to a groom who was standing waiting and marched over to his commanding officer and saluted before saying, "We were only a fairly short distance away, when we received the general's orders, so we dashed back. I presume that you wish to leave first thing tomorrow?"

"Yes Hugh, I thank you for your prompt action. I know nothing of this rebellion, although one legion should be ample to crush the rising, as it is down at the end of the mountainous range, that runs all the way to the south of this country."

"I think Centurion Thalius knows something about the leader of this rising, he was a gladiator and as you know some gladiators are not all muscle with no brains!"

Marcus eyed him shrewdly, "Are you referring to yourself? It is unlike you to blow your own bugle, but obviously he knows about fighting and we must be ready, as he has already taken a cohort that was sent out against him. Apparently he is creating quite a rising and many slaves are flocking to join his forces." He looked on around as they walked on towards their offices and spoke quietly, as if he did not want to be overheard. "This is the problem that Rome has with a weak emperor, we must ensure that there is harmony in the ranks, as that is how trouble starts, so it is up to you to speak to the centurions and make sure everyone is happy and that there is no discord or dissatisfaction in the lower ranks, because from what I have heard Senator Latitch wants to come in and ensure that the perpetrators of this uprising are dealt with most severely." Here he looked at Hugh and said that if the senator had his way there would be no mercy shown. I will leave it up to you." He then went into his own office.

Hugh spent most of the evening, packing his personal belongings, which were always kept in regular order. He then went to the senior officers in the legion and finally to the centurions to pass on the legate's wishes, trying to ensure that it was total harmony in the legion, so there could be no possibility of any desertion. He finally was satisfied and went to bed knowing that he had only a short time for any sleep. He woke early, but knew that he had not really had a decent night's sleep and he hoped that his tiredness did not show on his face. The legion marched by, although they bypassed his room and took the mountainous range way, which went out on the mountain range to Salerno to the south. His own chariot driver was a young centurion but who was from a very influential family, who had many connections and was obviously someone who hoped to go far. The man's name was Kreol, and as Hugh boarded the chariot he said, "Morning sir, how long will the march to Salerno take?"

"I understand it would normally take five days, but Legatus Marcus Anthony wants us to try to do it in four, although I am not really sure that is very wise, because we need to be in good fighting form at the end of the march. However there are a lot of reasons for quelling this uprising as soon as possible. Have you heard anything from your family connections?"

"Not really sir, although the family has some connections with a Vinter in the area, although there is no trouble, or not that we know of." He looked at Hugh as if he expected some more information.

Hugh considered that it would be not wise to trust the lad with his misgivings about Senator Latitch, as he did not feel totally confident about sharing his concern with this young man, he kept quiet, although some of his worries must have shown on his face, as Centurion Kreol said, "You look troubled sir, is it about the uprising?"

"No!"

He thought that he would steer the conversation away from these difficult subjects. "I was more concerned about my wife who is expecting again, or at least she may be, so please do not tell everybody yet."

"That's great news, I believe that you already have one, so obviously you intend to have a large family?"

"If possible centurion," replied Hugh, "but my position in the army may not allow me as much time with my wife and children as I would like. He then kept quiet, occasionally remarking about the well-kept fields and countryside that they were passing through. By the end of that day they had covered at least one quarter of their journey, which meant that they were travelling as quickly as the legate had wished.

During the next day their progress was slowed by a fairly common problem; one of the large baggage carts that was pulled by four steady horses came to an abrupt holt when the axel broke, causing a considerable delay, as the cart slewed across the main road and the only weapons that were carried like bundles of arrows were sent cascading over the road. While these items were picked up and redistributed onto the other wagons, as the break of the axel would take a considerable time. Legatus Marcus Anthony decided that they would continue and hopefully the wagon would be repaired by the driver and his two assistants who obviously had to stay behind while the legion pressed on. It did give Hugh the opportunity to see Thalius, who was travelling only a short distance away. He seemed quite cheerful and mentioned that he had not heard any complaints that the travel was too fast, although Hugh noticed that some of the new recruits were complaining about their blistered feet. Hugh smiled to himself, remembering the new equipment that he had been given when he joined the army, particularly the sandals, which had been mended with hard new leather binding, that needed to be softened up. This was often done by just continuous work or by people who knew about leatherwork. He could soften it by using mutton felt. That day's march was very successful, despite the hold up, they stopped and Legate Marcus Anthony instantly came over and showed Hugh where they were on the large map. His centurion/driver mentioned that he had heard that some of the senators wished to see some of the punishments that would be ordered against any captured rebels. This piece of information was of great interest to Hugh, who asked if Kreol knew who was behind it. "I am not very sure sir, but I heard that Senator Latitch was amongst the group of senators who wanted to see severe punishments, which would act as a deterrent to any other rebels."

When Hugh went for dinner that evening he was told that all the senior officers in the legion would be having a meeting to discuss their tactics. After his meal he went to the meeting, it was being held in the open area outside the legate tents. Marcus Anthony made a dramatic entrance and he carried some blocks of wood, these he arranged on the ground and Hugh noted that each was a different size and was marked with numbers that obviously corresponded to cohorts of groups of chariots. He laid them down, meticulously ensuring that everybody knew where he was to be positioned and what weapons were to be used. He told the men, "Now, hopefully we will arrive in the evening just outside Salerno, which many of you know is on the side of a hill, now we will be at an obvious disadvantage in having to attack up hill, but we will not follow the orthodox procedure. I will take the central cohorts," here he pointed to two large slabs of wood, "I want you to advance with just sword and javelin but they'll be followed by bow men, who will fire a folly of arrows over their heads. Now after each sword show has thrown three javelins I would like the cohorts to retreat back down hill, yet not breaking ranks." He looked up at his officers, who nodded with their agreement all wondering what would come next. "Now while they retreat, I would like the charioteers to advance on either side of the retreating cohorts, somewhat like the head of a bull, with the charioteers being the encircling horns; this will encourage an attack. The charioteers will then crush the attack against the stationary cohorts!"

"What a brilliant idea," said one of the younger tribunes.

"They will not be expecting that sir, it is an excellent idea, something that is not in the normal training book." Hugh knew the speaker, who often would often suck up sycophantically to his commanding officer; some of the other senior officers glanced at

Hugh and rolled their eyes. It was as much as Hugh could do to stop himself from smiling, because this tactic was one that the legate had obviously borrowed from reading General Priam's notes. Those very notes that he had made to General Priam's dictation when they had been in Londinium before they entered the galley, which brought them back to Rome. There were quite a few questions, mainly concerning what would be done to any captured soldier. "They should be treated with respect, after all they could be Roman citizens, if there is any punishment it would have to be ordered from the emperor, or certainly someone with his authority, that exceeds my power." As he said these words a cold feeling of premonition ran down Hugh's back, although there was no wind.

Legate Marcus Anthony kept on speaking, telling about how they should capture any groups of prisoners, who would be taken back to Rome under guard, where they would be sentenced. He continued speaking and the words were only half listened to by Hugh, until the name of Senator Latitch was mentioned. It appeared that the Hangmen's Dilemma was coming to Salerno, obviously after the battle simply to deal with the prisoners. Now Hugh wondered what fate he had in store for them, obviously nothing pleasant ever happened if Senator Latitch was behind it. The main thing ended and Hugh talked to the other officers who like him, could be in a chariot and would see a lot of fighting, not that this worried Hugh, as fighting was his trade. He wandered back to his own tent, but decided to check on how the other men who would be fighting with him felt about this development; particularly he wanted to talk to Thalius. Fortunately most of the men were still up and were talking about the battle that was coming up in a few days, sure enough when Hugh spoke to the second group of soldiers, one of them was Thalius, so he singled him out and with a nod of his head indicated that he would like to have a chat in private. Most of the soldiers, centurions and the officers knew that Thalius was a very good friend of Hugh's, even this fact was known to Legate Marcus, so nobody thought anything special about it. "Do you know who is coming after the battle Thalius," asked Hugh?

"Well I can guess, just by reading the expression on your face. Needless to say it is Senator Latitch, am I not right?"

"You certainly are my friend. Presumably you have heard that he is probably going to sentence the prisoners we capture, I wonder what horrors are in store for them, because there is no mercy where that piece of misery is!" Eventually feeling slightly better that someone he knew and trusted shared his belief, he went to bed and slept very well, not worrying at all about the battle they were facing.

Eventually after they marched tiredly they reached the outskirts of Salerno, during the fourth evening since leaving the barracks in Rome. At least half a days march before they arrived all were told that their approach should be kept fairly quiet, so all the moving carts were well greased with mutton fat and even many of the large horses had leather bags strapped around their feet so that they would not make too much noise. Although when they arrived at the base of the hill on which Salerno stood, they realised that the precautions were unnecessary as there was a large commotion from the town, which could be heard from quite a long way away. At a meeting with Marcus Anthony, it was realised that all the commotion came from the tavernas in the town where many of the rebel forces were misbehaving atrociously, becoming drunk and obviously behaving like many rebels do, to increase the population by lifting any girl's skirt, regardless of their age. It was fairly obvious that the battle would be easy for them to win, provided that they stuck to their plan. Hugh knew that fighting a crowd of people who had been drunk the previous night was not difficult, although a person with a sore head could be very aggressive. Mind you they were often uncoordinated. Deciding to take their possessions for the forthcoming battle, and await the dawn, everybody was restless, although this was possibly a good sign, much of the time was spent on ensuring that weapons were sharp, arrows were straight, javelins were sharp and their throwing thongs were securely strapped around the wrists of the soldiers.

Just before daylight, Hugh looked at some of the preparations that had been taken outside the town, he was sure that he could see large lengths of straw rolled into circular lengths, which would be set on fire and rolled down the hill at the attacking legion. The light was really clear enough in the half-light before dawn, so he asked where were the young centurions who had keen eyesight to look and tell him what he saw. After a young centurion had looked intensively at the objects that Hugh had indicated, he confirmed Hugh's suspicion. Therefore, Hugh made a sudden decision and ran back to Legate Marcus Anthony and after a quick conversation he received a go ahead for the plan that he had devised. He dashed around to the senior officers in charge of the two cohorts and they selected heavy wooden spikes about four cubits long hammered into the ground behind the campus and said that when they retreat they should retreat behind the hammered in iron spikes, that would prevent the roll down of burning straw from breaking up the ranks. After a few long moments the challenging bugles went in the air! This meant that the battle was beginning and all of the noise from the tavernas stopped, as they realised that they now had to fight the legion from Rome that was spread out beneath them at the base of the hill. It was obvious that some of the troops belonging to Spartacus were wide awake, even though some of the rebels were shaking each other awake to fight the battle. Eventually all the legion was in readiness and the troops lead by Spartacus began their assault, the calm morning air being torn asunder by the blast of trumpets and by the flash of fire, as the rolls of straw bales was set alight and were pushed down towards the attacking legion. As if they did not realise their peril, bowmen from the legion stepped in front of the first line of troops and fired three arrows apiece, before retreating with the front ranks to shelter behind their iron spikes, which Hugh had carefully positioned. The iron spikes did their job and prevented the burning straw bales from breaking up the centre of the attacking legion. Although the heat was initially fearsome, it soon died down, aided by water thrown on the bales by many of the soldiers and made ready for the attack. The rest of the battle went according to the plan that had previously been worked out and many of the rebel soldiers were captured by the encircling chariots. This effectively finished the rebellion lead by Spartacus and the important thing that now transpired was how the prisoners that were taken in the battle were dealt with.

The problem confronting Legatus Marcus Anthony was how to deal with the rebels, all his previous campaigns had been against opposing armies who either fought to their death or surrendered to the Roman force, when they were given the choice of fighting for the Romans, after undergoing training and swearing allegiance to the Roman Empire, or being taken as a captive and serving out the rest of their life on the galley's rowing benches. Marcus Anthony was forestalled in his decision by the unexpected arrival of Senator Latitch, whose appearance took everybody by surprise, as the Hangman's Dilemma stepped from behind his customary bodyguards. The small man strutted like a rooster to stand in front of Marcus Anthony and presented him with a scroll and said in loud ringing tones, 'This scroll gives me the authority to deal with the prisoners as I see fit, you will notice that it has the cartouche of Emperor Nero, that gives me the authority to deal with these rebels, but I will be lenient. We only want Spartacus, who will be crucified and all the other rebels will serve out the rest of their lives on the galley rowing benches.' This announcement took everybody by surprise, as they all knew that although crucifixion was a painful way to die yet, they were shocked by what happened next! Suddenly from amidst the prisoners who were all seated on the ground, when one man rose to his feet and declared, 'I am Spartacus.' Only to be followed by another man who did exactly the same thing. Suddenly all the prisoners seemed to be claiming that they were Spartacus. A wicked smile played over the hangman's dilemma's face,

"Crucify them all!"

All of the legion's senior officers looked aghast. Realising that they would be expected to carry out this most unpleasant punishment, they automatically looked at Marcus Anthony, who rallied and came to their defence, "You can not expect my men to carry out such a task, there is nothing on the scroll from the Emperor to that effect." This momentarily left Senator Latitch speechless, but he swiftly recovered and said, "However, your men can supply the crucifixes and my men will carry out the task. I will have each prisoner crucified from here on the road back to Rome, at every hundred paces along the road to Rome." Marcus Anthony then said, "We have just fought a battle, although I can spare a couple of my craftsmen to help you in this business, but do not expect any assistance from my soldiers." Many of the other senior officers breathed a sigh of relief at this announcement, they were very grateful not to be part of this most unpleasant duty. After the battle he decided to go amongst his men and thank them for the part that they played in the victory and also to check on any of the casualties. He was delighted to learn that there were no serious injuries and generally spirits were high. Most of the men were very grateful that their commander had handled the situation, although feeling that Marcus Anthony had made a deadly enemy even though Senator Latitch had plenty of enemies, he thought that he would like to be the person who administered the justice to Senator Latitch. On his rounds he came to Thalius who naturally smiled and asked, 'Do you have any idea of what are next assignment might be?'

'I suppose we will meet up with the General again and then sail to Judea, now that this unpleasant task has been performed.'

He then thought about the despatch that Marcus Anthony had shown him the previous day, he turned back to Thalius and said, 'I believe that a couple of legions have already sailed for Judea, so hopefully much of the fighting will already have been completed.'

'I would not be so sure about that,' exclaimed Thalius. 'You remember what I told you about the Jews, they are a very stubborn people and this new belief that some of them hold is most remarkable, they believe that the man who was crucified in Jerusalem was the son of the god that they believe in!'

'That doesn't really make sense,' replied Hugh, 'Surely a mortal man can not be a god?'

'I know, but they have strange beliefs and as I told you they are remarkably stubborn, I have also been told that they believe that this man has risen from the dead.' When he saw the surprised look on Hugh's face he chuckled and said, 'I know it's all very strange, but you will meet these people when we go to Judea.' However, Hugh did not have quite so long to wait because when they started on the march

114

back towards Rome on the very next day, the road was horribly marked by crucified individuals, many of whom were still alive and obviously in considerable distress, some of them actually called out to the legion, who were marching past, as they were dying of thirst and their wounds and some of them were having the ghastly experience of being eaten alive by the crows and seagulls. Having their eyes pecked out was most unpleasant for the passing legion. These men had all been gladiators and this was a very bitter end to their lives. Unfortunately the line of crucifixes continued for most of the day and it was a relief to come to the end of the crucified men and shortly afterwards they made camp beside the road and Hugh went to a meeting of all the senior officers. This meeting was addressed by Marcus Anthony, who told them that they would go to Naples and not return to their barracks, he went on to explain that General Priam would march the other two legions directly to Naples, so that there would be no chance of them seeing family or friends before they departed. They continued on their way towards Rome, and it was said that all roads lead to Rome, but when they were then in sight of the great city a most unusual sight met their eyes. Hugh was in his chariot at the head of the legion and he was most surprised to behold what was an unmistakable crucifix, although this person had been crucified upside down, out of interest he indicated to his driver that he wished to see the person up close, so they drove closer and Hugh could see the man was still alive, although only just. Hugh climbed down from the chariot's footplate and went over to read the sign that had been attached to the base of the upside down crucifix, it said 'On this is Petros who claimed he was the leading disciple of Jesus, the Jew that was crucified in Jerusalem.' The sight of blood was nothing new to Hugh but this sight really made his insides churn around. He could just see the party of people who had committed the crucifixion and he could make out Senator Latitch in the back of the wagon, who was still laughing about what he had ordered his men to do. Whether or not it was because his son had the same name, or just because of the callous behaviour of the Senator, Hugh was all ready and it took all his willpower to stop himself, charging after the Senator whom he really hated. He was brought was back to his senses by a groan from the dying man, who Hugh noticed had large and callused hands, as if he had once been used for hauling ropes. He crouched down beside the dying man and asked, "Why were you crucified upside down?"

"Because, I was unworthy," croaked the man, "to be crucified like the saviour, who I will now meet." With that he died.

Part Four

"The Sky Palace – Masada"

The legion turned away from Rome, following Hugh down the Roman road back to Naples. They had been marching all day, so Hugh had been ordered to try and find a farm where they could camp overnight. Just over the next hill he saw two large encampments where the other two legions were encamped, he recognised the standard over General Priam's tent, and ordered his charioteer to turn off the road and make camp. He stepped off the footstep of his chariot and went to where Marcus Anthony was, "I presume I did the correct thing Sir, I should imagine that you wanted to speak with General Priam before we leave for Judea?"

"Once again you have proved your worth, that is exactly what I wished. When you have all camped and had a bite to eat, we will go and see the General and find out what he intends."

Hugh was quite surprised but also delighted to be chosen by Marcus Anthony and go to see General Priam. The General was waiting for them inside his large tent, where a map of the Mediterranean Sea was spread out on the table. When they had all gathered around the table, the General indicated the map and pointed to a place that was marked as Gaza. He yelled out, "This port is one of the old main ports that originally was built by the old Philistines, who once ruled parts of Judea, they were originally enemies of the Jewish people who finally put them down over hundreds of years ago. Now I believe that the first two legions have headed for Gaza, so the port will be very busy with their unloading the transport galleys. However, I believe that there is another port only a days march north of Gaza, that was built by King Herod the Great, which is comparatively new, so that is the port that I will use to unload." There were a few more questions, which the General answered. He told them that this part of the land was very fertile. He said, "The Jews referred to it as The Land of Milk and Honey, which was given to them by their god. We will see whether or not they were correct, because according to the maps, part of the country is desert and very inhospitable."

"Have you never been there General?" asked Marcus Anthony.

"No I have never been there myself, however as I am sure you will know, it is now apart of the Roman Empire, even if it is one part that we have a great deal of trouble with because the people who live there will not be subjugated and have even refused to allow the Roman Eagles into their main Temple area in Jerusalem." The meeting seemed to have finished and many of the senior officers from the other legions began to drift away. However, as Marcus Anthony and Hugh began to leave the tent, they were momentarily stopped as the General barked, "One moment Legatus, I would like to talk to your Tribune Hugh." Marcus Anthony was not sure whether he should depart; yet he decided to stay. "I am alright Legatus, Hugh will be alright with me and I am sure that he will be able to find his way back to your encampment, I am sure that you are familiar with the close connection that we have." Hugh stood waiting while Marcus Anthony the tent, until he was alone with the General. The General smiled at Hugh and said, "I would like you to stay with me, obviously not as a companion, because I have my own staff and you have duties to your own legion. Although I wish to ensure that you sail on the same galley as me and you can always be near to speak to me, particularly about the Jewish people and their strange beliefs."

"Certainly Sir, but may I make a request?"

"I might have guessed, as you always answer my request with a question."

"Well it's quite simple really, you see I have become very friendly with Centurion Thalius, he has taught me a lot about Judea and the Jewish people, so naturally I would like him to be with me, if that is possible Sir?" he added.

"Alright Hugh, I know you are on very good terms with him, after all your wives are both staying with my sister, so I will make arrangements for that with your Legatus." The General turned back to study his map, making Hugh realise that he was dismissed.

Hugh found that the General was as good as his word, because in the morning, Centurion Kreol came together with Centurion Thalius. Centurion Kreol said, "I have been instructed by Marcus Anthony to come and allow Centurion Thalius to drive your chariot. Although I am not surprised at this order, as I know you are old friends, but all I wanted to ensure was that you were not displeased with my driving Sir."

"No Centurion Kreol, I have no problem with your driving and have made sure that the Legatus in charge of our Legion has a very good reason for the change." Centurion Kreol walked away, looking very relieved and walking with a definite spring to his step. Thalius turned to Hugh and said, "That was very well arranged, was it entirely your own doing?"

"No Thalius, it was part of the General's request, well at least it was mainly the General's request." Hugh knew that he didn't have to say that to Thalius, who was delighted that they would be together once more. From then on Hugh and Thalius were together again and followed the now familiar route back towards the harbour at Naples. They also shared a tent or other sleeping quarters, like a barn or outhouse when this was possible.

Eventually they reached the harbour at Naples, where there were many galleys waiting to take all three legions to Judea. "Do you know how long it will take us to reach Judea Thalius?"

"I am not very sure, but I suppose it will depend on the wind, although I think in nine or ten days we will be there." They stayed that night in the same Taverna that was occupied by General Priam and many of the other senior staff. Bearing in mind that there were three legions, this meant that there were two other Legatus', as well as Marcus Anthony. Effectively this meant that all the other officers' outranked Thalius, as he was only a centurion, however he was very knowledgeable about Judea and therefore became, more acceptable, to most of the other officers and more importantly at ease with himself. He was sharing his room with Hugh and on the second morning that they were in the Taverna he looked out on the harbour where there was always plenty of activity. He called over to Hugh and asked, "Is that not Senator Latitch and his customary bodyguards?" Hugh looked out of the window and saw his enemy, strutting around and giving orders.

"By the Gods you are correct Thalius, I wonder if the General knows that he is here, because I do not remember him mentioning that he would be joining the party." Hugh therefore left Thalius and picked up his helmet, breastplate and sword, making himself more formally dressed, before going in search of the General. He found the General quite easily, as the General was in conversation with the harbourmaster and other port officials.

General Priam beckoned Hugh to join him and said, "You look troubled, what has upset you?"

"He is here General!"

The General actually smiled, "Presumably you are referring to Senator Latitch?" The question was purely rhetorical and did not require an answer, so the General continued to speak, "I know he is here, I did not have much warning myself, although I did manage to ask the harbourmaster to allocate a private galley for the Senator and gave him instructions that he should be taken to Gaza, rather than to sail with the main fleet to Caesarea where we will be going, so do not worry yourself about it." He then spoke very quietly, so that Hugh could only just hear him, "I don't want the wretched little man around us, although he will probably arrive in Jerusalem before us and may the Gods help those people who he crosses, as I am sure that all my careful instructions on how to treat rebellious subjects will be ignored or overruled. I feel sure that he has probably come with a pre-signed statement, which gives him authority over the Governor in Jerusalem." Hugh realised that their private conversation was over, as the General walked back to the waiting harbourmaster and mentioned in his normal commanding voice, "I will be ready to take my senior soldiers on the first galley tomorrow morning."

120

Hugh and Thalius were ready the next morning to board the galley, where the chariots were dismantled and taken on board, "Are the horses not coming with us?" asked Hugh.

"No Hugh, there is no need, apart from which there will be a herd of waiting horses for us in Caesarea and they will be far superior to the horses we have been using here, they are all from Abyssinia, which is to the south of Judea, where they breed exceptionally good horse flesh." They followed on board themselves and found that they had been allocated a small cabin, right next to the General's main quarters. The General's rooms were surprisingly sumptuous, particularly compared to the rooms that Hugh and the General had shared in their voyage back from Britain.

As they went for a walk around the galley, Hugh mentioned to Thalius, "Needless to say you will remember the voyage back from Britain, where you were on the rowing benches?" Thalius simply nodded his agreement, allowing Hugh to continue speaking what was on his mind. "I think that it would be very instructive for the soldiers, apart from being good exercise for them to use their muscles in rowing the galley. Although we will have to make sure that they are not treated like slaves, but I think the General will be accessible to the idea. As someone who used to row on the galley benches, what do you think about the idea Thalius?"

"I think it is an excellent idea, you see just rowing the galley uses all you muscles, not just the arms as many people think, but also the leg and back, if you do it correctly."

"All right Thalius," said Hugh, "I will put the idea to the General as soon as we set sail and see what he thinks about my idea." They continued their walk until the galley was full and ready to sail. Then they went below to their cabin where their evening meal was brought to them.

Early the next morning Hugh spoke to the General about his idea of keeping the men fit by working on the rowing benches. The General was rather surprised, but said to Hugh, "I might have expected you to come up with such a scheme, you are always one for keeping the soldiers fit, I will give the idea a try, but I will join in the first shift."

"Is that wise sir? I mean the effort may not be very good for your leg," responded Hugh.

"I have always made it a rule that I will never ask one of my soldiers to do something that I will not do myself."

This was said with such finality that Hugh realised it was pointless to try to pursue the argument, so he merely suggested, "I have ordered Centurion Thalius to take charge of the first shift, which we will try out after the midday meal."

"I will be ready with some of my other senior staff," responded the General.

Hugh spoke to Thalius about the General insisting on being in the first party, "So keep a close watch on the old guy, as I do not wish him to strain himself." After the midday meal, which was fairly small, possibly because the General made an order for it, some of the senior soldiers, including the General and Marcus Anthony, came to the remaining rowing benches, many of whom were looking very apprehensive about this idea, but led by the General, who had stripped down to his waist, they took their places on the rowing benches, much to the surprise of some of the slaves who had been replaced and now stood to watch. After only forty-five minutes, according to the waterclock, Thalius signalled to the drummer, who would beat out the rowing speed on his large leather skinned drum with small hammers. Thalius ordered a brief rest and ordered the General and some of his other senior staff to rest and be replaced, as they were showing signs of strain and beads of sweat were showing on their foreheads, quite apart from the sweat that was pouring down their backs and from under their armpits. They all seemed very grateful to be replaced and moved with the stiffness that normally comes with age, certainly not one that you would expect with soldiers. Thalius had spent some of his time instructing some of their senior staff in how to row, as many of the officers had no idea of the work that was normally done by slaves.

In his rooms that evening the General called Hugh back from a normal staff meeting and said, "You are quite right my boy, it is very good exercise. I am going to issue an order for all the galleys in the fleet to do the same, as it will keep all the soldiers fit, as well as building up a better understanding between the soldiers and the slaves." The General looked around to check that there were no others listening before he continued, "I have told all the other galleys to maintain close contact, particularly at night by keeping shell lamps in the rigging, so we will make sure that the Hangman's Dilemma becomes well in front of us and then we will steer slightly more north, so he has no idea that we are not going to Gaza, but heading for Caesarea." Hugh returned from the meeting in good spirits and said to Thalius, "The General likes the idea and is issuing orders for all of the fleet to do the same and he then told Thalius of everything that the General had said, particularly that Senator Latitch would be going alone to Gaza." Thalius simply smiled at Hugh, knowing that no reply was necessary. Hugh and Thalius kept up with the work of keeping all the soldiers doing a brief time on the rowing benches, as well as his own daily routine of sword practice, going through the standard 12 parries and cuts, as well as javelin practice, where a target was set up at the stern of the galley.

On the galley occupied by Senator Latitch and his small force, who all enjoyed good accommodation, as well as being fed well, Senator Latitch occasionally looked back at the rest of the fleet and noted that there was often comings and goings between the galleys, he was certain that this was to hold meetings between all the senior officers of all three legions. He mentioned this to the galley captain, who was a large brute of a man called Brutaus, who had no consideration for his slaves, and normally used far more than the other galley captains, and then threw the slaves, who were of no further use, to the sharks, which greatly amused everybody, particularly Senator Latitch. His name was appropriate, as he was a large man who was more like a bear. All his crew despised him, wishing him nothing but trouble and some of them had even tried to poison him, but obviously they had failed and when discovered their deaths had been most cruel. Naturally Senator Latitch liked the man and approved of his treatment of his crew, the Senator had even approved of his renaming of the galley, although renaming any seafaring vessel was considered bad luck. He had taken the vessel from the Greeks, who had named it

Artemus, after the Greek Goddess who came from the sea, in fact he had renamed the galley Venus, who was the same God but given a Roman name.

Brutaus was always very polite to the Senator, which was one of the reasons that the Senator approved of him. He constantly encouraged Brutaus to speed his galley on towards Gaza. Obviously Brutaus had not known that the other galleys were headed for Caesarea, a fact that he mentioned to the Senator.

"No captain, we are to sail to Gaza," stated the Senator categorically! On the third day after leaving Naples the wind blew them further south than they would normally go and they rounded a small island and the Senator demanded, "What island is that Captain Brutaus?"

"It is an island called Malta."

"Is that not the island where that interfering Christian came from, or was shipwrecked here?" asked the Senator.

"Possibly sir," replied Brutaus. Although in fact he had no idea of what the Senator was talking about, he wanted to sound more knowledgeable than he was, so he felt it best to agree. "We will sail north of that rock and continue east around the island, that will hopefully make certain that we have shaken-off the rest of the fleet." He proved to be right, as they did not see anymore of the main fleet led by General Priam.

On board the galley carrying General Priam and the senior soldiers, who still continued their training on the rowing benches, which was now practiced on most of the galleys. They sailed north of Malta and the same storm had made sure that they were now out of sight of the galley name *Venus* on which Senator Latitch was on board. Thalius pointed this out to Hugh saying, "That's great, we should not be seeing the Hangmen's Dilemma again."

"I only wish that you are correct, although I have a feeling in my guts that we will see the wretched little man again," replied Hugh. The voyage continued and although Hugh enjoyed the company of Thalius, as well as the regular meeting with the General and his other senior staff, he was glad when a lookout called out, "Land ahead!" The Captain of the galley, together with the rest of the fleet, had made a perfect landfall just off the coast of Caesarea. Theirs was the first galley to dock in the new harbour, that could accommodate two or three galleys at a time, the rest waited just a little of shore, until they were summoned into the dock, where they were very efficiently unloaded. Hugh was delighted to see that Thalius had been correct and there was a small herd of horses to meet the chariots, which were quickly assembled. Hugh was delighted with the new horses, particularly when they were allowed to choose the horses themselves. Hugh and Thalius walked amongst the horses and chose two that seemed to be a good pair and make a good team, as one was a stallion and the other a mare. By the time that they had harnessed the horses to the tarsal of their newly erected chariot, which had a newly greased wheels and axel, the 1st Legion was now ready to march, although the 2nd Legion was already unloaded from their galleys, while the 3rd Legion was still waiting in galleys off the coast.

The legion fell in on the Roman road that followed the shoreline south towards Gaza, where they knew that 4th and 5th Legions and Senator Latitch had already docked, this was as Thalius said the fastest way to reach the capital city of Jerusalem, despite it not being in a direct route, so effectively they were travelling down two sides of a right-angle triangle. Hugh asked, "Why can we not go overland, because it seems to be quite easy country?"

"Well it maybe here, but we do not know if there are any difficult areas, or large rivers," Thalius replied. "Well there are according to the maps that we have, which were originally drawn-up by the Greeks. They only mention one river called the River Jordan, which apparently flows from a large inland lake called Lake Kinneret, but it is not a big river and I believe that Lake Kinneret is below sea level."

"By the gods! Where on earth does it flow to?" asked Hugh.

"To a place where they say there is a sea, although it is an inland sea and apparently very salty, I have been told," said Thalius. They continued their discussion of this land called Judea, all the way towards Gaza, although they made camp just short of the town. Hugh went to a meeting in the General's tent, along with the other senior officers of the 1st Legion, who were then joined by the 2nd Legion, whose Legatus told the general that the 3rd Legion was on its way.

The General asked, "Has anyone met any of the native inhabitants of Judea yet?"

"Well, yes, Sir" said Hugh, "the man in charge of the herd of horses was a Jew and he seemed very nice, although he said it was just as well that we arrived today as he was not allowed to work tomorrow, because it is against their religious beliefs to work on the day they call the Sabbath, which is every seventh day or so I am told," he said this with raised eyebrows to the emphasise it strangeness.

"Yes I believe they have very strange beliefs, but we should allow for that, as I am sure you have all read my treatise on this?" He growled out this, looking enquiringly around him. There was a moment of silence and Hugh thought that it was obvious that some of the senior officers had not yet done so but clearly would make sure they did read the scrolls, at their earliest convenience. The meeting went well and they were all told to be kind to the local people and allow them their strange beliefs, provided that they did not interfere with the running of the Legion, but even if they did, the General emphasised that it was always possible to circumvent this problem, because the people were now under Roman Law. When Hugh returned with Thalius to his tent, Thalius asked him how the meeting had gone.

'Very well,' replied Hugh. He then went on to explain to Thalius everything that the General had spoken about, including the details of his instructions about how to treat other people who existed under Roman Law, of how some senior officers had not read his scrolls, which Hugh had worked on with the General in Londinium. They both exchanged meaningful looks at each other and burst out laughing.

The next morning Hugh noticed that the other leaders had arrived, so they were soon ready to march on towards Gaza. It was only a short distance away and when they arrived they found the remaining galleys just about to leave. There was a sharp whistle blast, meaning that the General required Hugh to return to him. Soon Thalius swung the horses in a very tight circle, so that the left-hand wheel did not turn but simply swivelled on its axis and they were soon back beside the General. Hugh looked up at the General who was mounted on one of the white stallions, as he always chose a white stallion if possible. Hugh remembered his white horse back in Britain, which had thrown him when Queen Boadicea charged at him. The General wanted Hugh to order one of the remaining galley captains to come and talk to him, so Hugh signalled to Thalius to turn the chariots back towards the remaining galleys and they dashed off to find the captain. They soon returned with the galley captain on the footplate of the chariot, Hugh realised that the captain was amazed that he had been asked to see the General. Hugh led him to the General, calmingly telling him that all the General wanted was information, probably about Senator Latitch. Hugh waited for a while and then had to return the galley captain to his galley. The galley captain was in a far more cheerful mood and told Hugh all about his meeting and the strange behaviour of the Senator, "He was very insistent that he and his bodyguards travelled at the rear of the legions, but he insisted that he should speak to the Governor of Judea, at the Roman fortress in Jerusalem."

"That does not surprise me," said Hugh thoughtfully, "I bet he has another decree up his sleeve!"

"You seem to know him well," observed the galley captain.

"Yes, you could say that. We are old friends," he paused for a while and then continued, "Well friends is not the right word, enemies is closer."

After the captain went back to his galley, they turned the chariot around and took their place back with the legion, which was now heading towards Jerusalem.

They rode along in silence for a while until Hugh suddenly said, "This looks like a pleasant land, it is very warm yet not stuffy and we seem to be heading upwards from the coast, is Jerusalem very high?"

"Could well be, so I believe, it is possibly two thousand cubits above sea level," replied Thalius. "The land is very nice on the west side of the River Jordan, but on the other side it is desert, all sand and rock." They travelled eastwards for the rest of the day, chatting occasionally, mainly about their wives and children. All three legions made a very long procession, travelling through the land that was occasionally populated by small towns or villages where women or small children would often stare at the long procession of the passing soldiers. Some of the children even waved, particularly when their parents were not watching them and Thalius and Hugh waved back, smiling at the kids. One of the young boys was quite adventurous and even stroked one of their horses, during the brief stop. As he seemed very interested, Hugh leant over and smiled, lifting him into the chariot. Then he showed him all around, the weapons in their racks and of how Thalius made the horses gallop or trot, just by shaking or pulling on the reins. The little boy was very interested and gabbled something to Hugh.

"I do not know what you are saying little one?" he looked at Thalius and said, "What language is he speaking?"

"I believe it is a language called Hebrew," replied Thalius. "However nobody can read it, as it is all written back to front! Their laws are in the same language and they have a strange form of government, which is administered by their priests, you will probably remember, as I told you about a man whom they had crucified, although they allowed a known robber to go free."

Thalius shook his head, showing his incredulity. Hugh finally put the boy down in the small village where they stopped, after the boy had indicated and said in the Roman tongue, "My auntie lives here."

At the normal senior staff meeting that evening, Marcus Anthony said to Hugh, "Do you think you were wise in taking that little boy on board your chariot?"

"I do not see why you are questioning me about that Legatus. After all, the General told us to be courteous to the inhabitants of this land, apart from which I like small children, at least when they are not all noise at one end and none of your responsibility at the other end." He laughed to emphasise his jest and that he was not being rude to his commanding officer.

"I heard that," growled General Priam. "I think that Hugh is quite correct, Hugh should not be told off. In fact I would like to see some more friendliness shown to the people of Judea." The meeting continued in the normal way that the General's staff meetings were conducted. Hugh returned to talk to Thalius before they went to sleep, they were camped around a small village just on the outskirts of

Jerusalem, which was over the reach to Judea to the east, it was visible in the dusk, as they could see many torches burning in the city, where there was obviously some form of a riot going on.

"What do you think is happening down there?" asked Thalius?

"I am not sure," replied Hugh. "Whatever is happening is certainly not good news, I would not be surprised if the Hangman's Dilemma is at the bottom of the trouble." Regrettably he was perfectly correct, Senator Latitch was in the Roman garrison called The Fortress Antoninia, proclaiming that the soldiers would massacre any Jewish people who were on the street after curfew.

The next morning the General ordered his troops to be visible above the valley, in which Jerusalem was situated. Hugh and Thalius had a good view of the walled city, where there was still rioting and some fighting going on, although a small contingent of rebels had broken through and was seen to be leaving the city and heading to the east and then turning south where there was noticeably a large amount of sand dunes, looking most inhospitable.

The General ordered Marcus Anthony and a legatus of one of the other legions and his charioteer to follow them down to the nearest gateway of the city, as well as Hugh and Thalius, much to Hugh's surprise. The General mounted his horse and led the small party down to the city, where they were met by the Roman Governor of the city, followed closely by Senator Latitch with his customary bodyguards. The Roman Governor, a man called Pontius Pilate came forward to meet the General and said, "I am glad that you arrived and probably saw the riot that was led by a group of people who called themselves Zealots, I believe that they have gone on the road that leads to Jericho and the Salt Sea, which is also Dead Sea, as nothing grows there."

He was pushed unceremoniously aside by Senator Latitch who demanded, "I order you to follow them with all your three legions." Pontius Pilate looked almost apologetic at the General and was grateful when the General gave him a brief smile.

"It is not your place to give me orders Senator Latitch," barked the General in a most unfriendly manner. "I am going to follow the men, simply because it is my orders and not because you wished me to." The General was about to turn away when he was interrupted.

"I do not care what your orders are," shouted the Senator. "You will do as I say. I have here a proclamation by Emperor Nero, that gives me authority about everything that goes on in Jerusalem, or in the whole of Judea!" The General ignored him and remounted his horse and beckoned his small party to follow and they rode back to where all three legions were gathered.

"Was it wise to speak to Senator Latitch like that General? After all, I think he will make a pronouncement against you to the Emperor," said Hugh.

"I do not care what the wretched little man does," was the reply. "My sister once threatened to mutilate him and I will do the same myself, if he ever orders me again." Hugh felt sure that the General was enjoying himself, he was also sure that the General smiled briefly at him. They were all ordered to ensure that they had plenty of water and all their water carriers were filled up, as they were now marching through a barren part of the land.

"Should we not ask for water from the city," enquired Marcus Anthony?

"There is no need, as this valley has its own water course, that I believe flows into the city, although you can take fresh water from the stream before it enters the city," said the General. All the soldiers made sure that they had full water carriers and that their horses had all been refreshed, before they once again set off around another small village travelling fairly steeply downhill.

After Hugh and Thalius had watered the horses, as well as making sure that their water containers were full, they climbed back into their chariot and were soon at their place in the front of the 1st Legion. They headed southeast on the same road that the fleeing rebels had taken, which was a fairly steep road in very inhospitable country. The journey was made more difficult by the strong sunshine rebounding off sand and rocks almost blinding them. They were glad that they had plenty of water, as it was necessary to keep drinking. That evening they had just passed a small group of houses, only containing a Taverna that the local people referred to as an inn. Hugh and Thalius set up their shelter for the night; this was not really a tent, as it certainly did not look like raining, but was more of a bivouac. "I see what you mean about this country Thalius," said Hugh. "It is completely different this side of the valley called Kedron, where Jerusalem is built."

"Yes it certainly is," replied Thalius, as he wiped the sweat out of his eyes.

"Do you think the rebels will be in Jericho, where this road apparently goes to?"

"I am not really sure old friend, apparently Jericho is one of the oldest cities in this country, but apparently it does not have any walls now."

"Why, what happened to them?" asked Hugh.

"It is a very strange story Hugh, but the Jewish people believe that their god made the walls fall down, after some of their army had marched around the walls for a few days and then blew their trumpets, causing the walls to fall down. If you can believe such a story Hugh."

The next day they continued on their way and the path became very difficult and in some places only one chariot at a time could pass, making the pursuit of the Zealots more difficult. Eventually they came out of a rocky defile, seeing before them a very pleasant city, with small pools and jacaranda trees surrounding it. It looked very pleasant and fertile after the desert lands they had crossed, there was also a small river flowing through the valley, that was surrounded by fairly high cliffs. In particular one just above Jericho, in which there were lots of small caves, some of which seemed inhabited by monks in dark hooded robes. All of this made Jericho seem more pleasant. They watered their horses and were refilling their water containers, which had nearly all been drunk by the horses. At that moment a delegation came from the city. The General having seen their approach, had ordered Marcus Anthony as well as Hugh and Thalius to follow him to meet the group. A spokesman from the delegation came forward and spoke to the General, "If you are looking for the Zealots you have best go down to the Dead Sea. I believe they have gone to the Palace

Masada, Herod's Sky Palace down by the Dead Sea." The General simply thanked the man for this information, before turning to Marcus Anthony and telling him to prepare to head down to the place called Masada.

"We will be ready to leave first thing in the morning General, if that is alright, but my lads had a very difficult journey down from Jerusalem and they need a good rest as do the other two legions who are still on their way," said Marcus Anthony.

"Of course, Legatus. As you will know, I never press my troops too hard," said the General.

Hugh and Thalius pitched their small tent and then went for a brief walk around the City of Jericho, before Hugh had to go to the senior officers meeting with the General. They wandered through the old city and saw the river Jordan, which was not very deep and led to the salt sea that was giving a red glow from the sunset in the west. "Do you know anything about this palace called Masada?" Hugh asked Thalius.

"Not really Hugh, except that it is meant to be very difficult to reach, I believe you will probably hear more at the General's meeting this evening," suggested Thalius. They wandered back to the tent and as Thalius entered, there was a shrill double blast on the whistle meaning that Hugh had to depart for the Senior Officers meeting with the General. The meeting was very informative, and there was a Tribune from the small force of Roman soldiers in Jerusalem at the meeting. He said, "Masada is almost a full days march down on the west side of the Dead Sea, but it is on a separate rock, that is severed from the main cliff." The rest of the meeting was also very interesting, as many ideas were discussed on how to reach it, although nothing was really decided until they came within sight of the palace and saw what was necessary.

"I think we may have to build a ramp to allow a siege engine to be pushed to the top," observed the General. Just then there was a minor disturbance just outside the General's tent, when Senator Latitch marched in. He scornfully looked about him and was about to speak when he was forestalled. "What in the name of all the gods do

132

you mean by just walking in on my private meeting?" snarled the General. "If you do anything like that again you will pay dearly for it, I am ordering Legatus Marcus Anthony to have you taken away and kept outside of Jericho, in fact you will now be kept under guard and no scroll that you write will be allowed out." The senator's face blushed, as Legatus Marcus Anthony and one of his Tribune frog marched the Senator out of the tent. One of the Senator's bodyguards began to draw his sword, but his wrist was grabbed by Marcus Anthony and although he was a big man, he had enough wit to realise that he was totally outclassed by all the senior soldiers who were watching in the tent.

Hugh had plenty to tell Thalius that night when he went back to his tent. "I would have like to have seen that. What did the Hangman's Dilemma do?" asked Thalius.

"Like I said," replied Hugh, "all the blood drained from his face and he was marched out of the tent. He is now being kept under guard," much to Thalius's surprise and relief.

Hugh said, "I will sleep easier tonight, knowing the senator is under guard."

"I agree with you Hugh, but will the General be in trouble for doing that to the senator."

"Probably Thalius, I reckon that the General has been getting into trouble for years, although, he only wanted this to be his last campaign before he retired and go back to living with his sister and to manage the family estates."

The next morning having filled all their water containers and made sure all the horses were well watered, before re-harnessing them to their chariot's braces, they then climbed into their chariots and headed off south down along the west shore of the Dead Sea.

It was very hot although it was only morning; the cliffs on the right seemed foreboding, although there was no trace of life. The wheels of the chariots ran cleanly over the white sand, which they realised, consisted mainly of salt not ordinary sand. They both had the feeling that this would be a long campaign, despite the fact they were pursuing a small band of rebels. From what they knew about the Jews and the Zealots, who were very dedicated and fearless, they knew that

133

this was not going to be easy. In an attempt to lighten the feeling of dread Hugh said, "At least we will end up with a decent suntan."

As they travelled down beside the Dead Sea, Hugh felt that he would try to brighten the atmosphere by asking about the Dead Sea. He asked Thalius, "What do you know about this Dead Sea, which to me seems more like a large lake."

"From what I have heard, it is very salty and it is impossible to swim in it, although you can float on your back but you must not allow the water to touch your eyes, because it stings like a scorpion and you have to use fresh water to clean the salt from your eyes."

"Sounds like a very unusual experience," remarked Hugh. "It sounds like you are floating in treacle." He threw a loose stone into the water yet to his surprise it made a normal splash. When they had travelled further they stopped to water the horses, as well as to have a drink themselves, because it was very hot. Hugh used the time to walk down to the water's edge and scoop a handful of it. To his surprise it seemed just like ordinary water, until he tasted it and then he realised how salty it was, he pulled a grim expression!

"Presumably you didn't like it," said Thalius.

"No, it was absolutely disgusting," responded Hugh.

"It is not surprising that nothing grows down here," replied Thalius.

"Well there does seem to be something further on, just at the base of the cliff," said Thalius, as he pointed to some palm trees and some buildings, that he could just see further ahead. As they continued the buildings gradually came into view, it was a small group of huts, built around a small area where some date palms were grown, obviously around a fresh water spring. The General called a halt by this small oasis and said, "We will make camp here, because the Palace of Masada is high up and on the cliff above where we are now." Everybody looked upwards to their right and saw the Palace of Masada high up on the cliff. They could also see a path that led up to Masada, obviously in a series of zigzags, which could only be travelled by one or two men abreast, even then it would be difficult to climb. This made the Palace of Masada very difficult to assault and break into. As they were making camp, Hugh said, "It looks very difficult to get up there, in large enough numbers to make an assault on the fortress."

"It will be interesting to hear what the General's staff meeting decides this evening," observed Thalius.

"By the look of the walls that surround the palace, which would seem very large in area, as well as the large gate on the entry, I think that we will have to build a ramp, as the General suggested. But exactly how we do it is quite a problem."

At the General's staff meeting, the General had many ideas to be discussed, but it was decided to reconnoitre the area before anything was decided. During the meeting there was a commotion and two of the guards marched into the General's tent, with one of Senator Latitch"s bodyguards, who had been trying to escape, with a scroll addressed to Emperor Nero. Everybody looked at the General, who had taken the scroll and opened it. He read the scroll out; his face became angrier as he read it. It was not surprising, because the scroll read:

'To Emperor Nero, the Divine and Beloved of the Gods,
from Senator Latitch, Your servant in Judea, who quelled the uprising in Jerusalem.

Some of the rebels, who called themselves Zealots, have escaped and travelled down to the Dead Sea and are now in The Palace of Masada. I have travelled with the three legions commanded by General Priam, who has forbidden me to inform you of this, as well as holding me hostage. He has only come down to the south because I insisted that these Zealots be captured. However, he is reluctant to follow my instructions. I therefore insist that he should be stripped of his rank and be returned to Rome, where he be tried by the Senate and yourself for committing treason'.

The scroll had the Emperor's cartouche on the bottom of the scroll. The General showed the scroll to all his senior officers and they were all as angry as the General. Hugh was surprised that the General did not strike off Senator Latitch bodyguard's head, which was something that he felt like doing, as did most of the other senior officers. The General simply told the guards to march the bodyguard back to Senator Latitch's compound and to double the guards and make sure that no message could be taken to the Emperor. He said, "I think I will write to the Emperor myself and tell him that all the trouble in Jerusalem was caused by the Senator, and also that the Zealots have caused all my three legions to follow to this cursed place, where we will actually experience great difficulty in breaking into the Palace of Masada. The cost of all the legions must be considered and we are not yet sure how to ensure that the Zealots can no further travel through your rule of Judea."

A scribe, who was sitting beside the General, wrote this message onto a scroll, sanded the parchment, rolled it into a scroll tube, after fixing the Emperor's cartouche onto the scroll and sealed it with hot wax. Once this had been sent, the General listened to everything his senior officers could decide about gaining entry to Masada. It was decided that before any decision could be realistically made, a complete reconnaissance of the area be made, complete with maps and drawings. Finally the meeting ended, with everyone knowing what tasks lay ahead.

When Hugh arrived back in his tent, Thalius asked him, "What was decided at the meeting, Hugh?"

"Well, we have to reconnoitre the area and make drawings, so that we can work out the best way to break into Masada. Are you any good at drawing, Thalius?"

"Well, I used to be reasonable, although I am no expert. In fact, it is a long time since I even drew anything!" He then looked at Hugh enquiringly.

"I am not, and I have never done anything like this before, but I sketched people's faces at the meeting. See if you can recognise any of them?"

Thalius took the drawings and after a while he said, "These are excellent Hugh, I can recognise all the people, obviously the general does not look pleased. Presumably it had to do with the bodyguard that is in the picture, he was one of the thugs that tried to assault us when we climbed Mount Vesuvius; I remember hearing a commotion shortly before you returned. Needless to say it was this animal who caused the problem."

"Yes, you are quite correct," Hugh said, then went on to explain about the rest of the meeting and of how they were expected to draw a detailed sketch of the cliffs surrounding Masada. "I am not very sure of how to go about drawing them, do you have any ideas?"

"Well I had a good look up at the cliffs when you went to the meeting, I think that if we follow the path that leads to Masada, and about three quarters of the way up we leave the path and climb over to the left, where there is a good place to sit and make a detailed observation of Masada and the rock face. Yet it would advisable to take a length of rope and tie ourselves together using an anchoring point, so that we could traverse to a more convenient place as the area looks difficult to climb."

"Um, I suppose it is worth a try, we have all day tomorrow and the day after tomorrow before the General requires a report, so I think we will do that." They continued to talk until it was very late. All that could be heard was, the occasional footfall of one the guards patrolling Senator Lattich's compound.

The next morning, after breaking their fast and doing their normal sword practice, Hugh and Thalius equipped themselves with plenty of rope, which they could easily carry over their shoulders, and found that it did not impede their climbing up the path towards Masada. They had almost reached the point where they would branch away from the main route, when they could see a commotion at the base of the cliff. They stayed still and listened intently to the argument that was between Senator Latitch's bodyguards and some of the soldiers who were on guard duty. It was apparent that Senator Latitch wanted his bodyguard to carry him up the slope toward Masada, but the guards were refusing, as they had not been given any instructions to allow the senator to go towards Masada. They sent a centurion over to the General's tent. The centurion came back and enquired, "Why did the senator want to approach the foot, as it was a difficult climb?"

One of his bodyguards replied saying, "The Senator will not be climbing himself, but wishes that we should carry him on a chair we have attached carrying poles to." The argument continued for quite a while and Hugh and Thalius could not clearly make out everything that was said, because everybody began shouting at one another, and in the confusion the General himself came over and shouted, "What is all the noise about?" After a long pause, when the centurion explained exactly what was happening, they could hear the General who directed himself at Senator Latitch and said, "With all due respect Senator, you cannot expect any of your bodyguards or my soldier to carry you up this pass. Surely you must realise that it is very dangerous and I would not expect one of my trained soldiers to climb it let alone to carry you. I therefore forbid this idea. I will consider your request, after my men have climbed the area themselves, but then and only if I feel it is safe for you. I feel it is sensible to make this judgement, because by the looks of your bodyguards they were not looking forward to the job." The argument died away as the General went back to his headquarters tent and Senator Latitch and his bodyguards returned to their compound. Hugh and Thalius continued up the cliff using one of the ropes over a very difficult stretch where there were only a couple of patches where they could only hang on by the fingers, as there was nowhere to gather any purchase for their feet. Eventually they reached the point they had been aiming to reach and they found, as Thalius had suggested, a good point to sit and sketch the complete area, including the top of the cliffs, as well as the part on which Masada had been build, that was on a sort of square, away from the rest if the cliff.

They were both out of breath when they hauled themselves into a reasonable sitting position. After his breathing had returned to normal Hugh took out a piece of parchment he had been carrying together with a piece of charcoal. He started drawing the palace and commented, "It is remarkably large and extremely well built. It must cover an area that is even larger than one of our legion's encampments, but I was wondering where they have their fresh water?

I am sure that the palace was prepared in advance, there must be large cisterns of water in there, as well as plenty of food already stored."

Hugh thought about this for a while, as he worked on the sketch. The only sounds were the scratching of the charcoal on the parchment, until he broke the silence by saying, "Yes Thalius I suppose you are correct, all of this was planned, probably before we arrived in Jerusalem." He continued drawing and then said, "I suppose I had better note how high the palace sits above the Dead Sea and our encampment. How high do you reckon we are?"

"I am sure we are at least 500 cubits above the Dead Sea," observed Thelius. "Although it is very difficult to be sure, because I believe it is so hot and it never rains, although the Dead Sea seems to hurt my eyes with the light reflecting on it."

They continued working on the drawings; Hugh doing the sketching with Thalius making occasional remarks, until they considered them good enough. Eventually they considered that they had plenty of detail of the palace of Masada fixed in there minds, so they made sure that the rope was securely tired around a rock outcrop that they could use again, before they climbed down. When they reached the sand at the base of the cliff, they saw that Marcus Anthony was waiting for them.

"I thought it must have been you two up there," commented Marcus Anthony, "needless to say you probably heard all the arguments between Senator Latitch and the General. It seems as if the senator must have instructed a messenger to be sent from Jerusalem," he said conversationally as he welcomed them back to the encampment. "As you can imagine the General is not very happy, he will have to wait here until we hear from Rome, although the situation of keeping three legions here, while there are only a handful of rebels holding the palace, seems absolutely ridiculous!"

"I agree with you sir," said Hugh. "You will be pleased that we have now very good drawings of Masada complete with the estimates of the height above the Dead Sea, as well as a full knowledge of the cliff face, which we climbed to make the drawing."

"I think that you have done well, particularly as the sun must have been shining from this salt water sea, although it is only a lake. I sent a skeleton party out around the rest of the valley and they found there were some old ruins of an ancient settlement that is half buried by rocks at the far south of the lake. There must have been a complete settlement here, although it must have existed before our empire. Possibly it may date back to the Greeks or before, it could be ancient Egyptian as they had a great empire that dates back many life times, before we were born."

Hugh and Thalius returned to their tent, glad to be out of the bright sunlight. "From what Marcus Anthony was saying and from the exchange of words that we heard from the General, it would seem he is in a very angry mood," Thalius remarked.

"Well, I think that the General will be pleased with what we have achieved. Although we need to examine the various opportunities that are available to the general," said Hugh thoughtfully.

"What do you mean," asked Thalius.

"I am trying to think ahead," said Hugh. "Why, so what do you think the General wants us to do?"

"Surely he needs the drawings in order to work out how we are going to break into Masada?"

"Oh yes, I understand what you are suggesting. Presumably you think that we should try to work out a way to break in to or destroy Masada. I think we are considering an almost impossible task. It may be within bow range from on top of the cliffs , but bows are of no use against solid stone buildings, even if we used fire arrows, there is nothing to burn," said Thalius to Hugh as they looked on in despair.

"No, you are perfectly correct, when this place was built, it was designed to be impregnable, the obvious solution would be a small force, possibly a cohort of soldiers, but that option is not open to the General, thanks to the bloody Senator. That's why, I think the only solution is to build an enormous ramp and haul up a siege engine to break down the door," Hugh commented. "Although I would not like to suggest it, as that would take forever!"

Hugh sat and thought while Thalius rested during the hottest part of the day. It was just after the normal midday meal, which was of fruit that had been brought down from Jericho. Hugh lay and thought, and decided to go and test out floating in the Dead Sea.

As he walked to the sea, which Marcus Anthony had told them was really a lake, he contemplated the meeting that was due tomorrow evening and wondered whether he should suggest building the ramp, although he had gained the notion from the General, he had no wish to steal the idea. However, he shortly waded into the sea, which to his surprise did not feel very different from ordinary water, although he could feel that it was somehow different. He had remembered about what Thalius said about not allowing the water to enter his eyes, so he tried dabbing a few drops on his eyes and gasped at the burning sensation that it created. Fortunately his eyes filled with tears, which washed away the water from the Dead Sea and after a few moments he felt that he could see again, possibly even more clearly. Although he thought that it could not really be wise to suggest this as a medical treatment, he thought it and the idea was already in his mind. He gradually lowered himself into the sea and even though it was only just above his knees he lay on his back and was surprised to realise that he was floating on the water, which did not fully cover him. It was fairly pleasant lying in the water, which was warmer than usual. He was used to swimming in very cold water, as when he had been a young lad and he had lived in Britain. He realised after a while that his hands were beginning to feel uncomfortable, particularly where he had grazed the skin, when he had been climbing up the cliffs, so after a short period of laying in the water and propelling himself by swimming with his hands, but carefully, so as not to make any splashes. He finally stood up and walked out of the water, and almost immediately he felt that he needed to brush his back, as the water was evaporating in the bright sunlight, leaving white crystals on his skin. He was about to call for some water, when he noticed a small stream of clear water that must have come from this small pool where all the legions took their fresh water. He busied himself for a while in making a crescent shaped dam using the large stones and small ones in between them to create a small paddling pool. It was large enough for him to lay down in it and wash all the salt water from his body, after which he felt a lot better and walked back to his tent and joined Thalius in lying down. After a while Thalius spoke to him, "I was half asleep when you left the tent, where did you go to?"

"I went for a swim, well really a float in the Dead Sea, although I remembered what you told me and know that it was quite unlike anything else I have ever done. It was quite remarkable and then I built a small dam in the stream that runs down from where we take our fresh water, you know the pool that is surrounded by palm trees at the base of the cliffs. One of the other things that I realised is that the abrasions on my hands started to sting, wherever the water from the Dead Sea penetrated my skin, although it has now started to heal the sore places, if you would look at my hands, and also where I must have rubbed my legs on the rocks, there is a new growth of skin covering the places." He held up his hands so that Thalius could inspect them.

Thalius looked at his hands and said, "You know I think you are correct Hugh, perhaps this salt sea has special properties that we never realised!"

Hugh spoke to Thalius about his other thoughts, about the ramp being the only realistic solution to break into Masada. Pleased to change the subject and speak about something that was always close to his mind, as well as being something that he shared with Thalius, he said. "I wonder how the girls are?" referring to Rosanna and Lydia, and the children.

The men talked about the other things, like their old settlement that Marcus Anthony talked about at the end of the salt sea. They talked for a while and then as the sun began to disappear behind the large cliffs to the west they thought it was about time for the evening meal and went over to the mess area.

In the mess area they were joined by one of the medical orderlies, who was attached to the legion and who asked Hugh, "I was told that you went into the Dead Sea today and have experienced strange healing properties from the water, is that correct?"

"Yes, I did," he then displayed the minor injuries that had been cured by going into the water. "Possibly this lake, or the sea has special qualities of healing. Although I think you may wish to examine some of the other people who had been into the water, although I don't think that any of them went in as much as I did."

"Yes I think you may be correct, do you know how long we will be here? Because I have plenty of other worries, particularly about making sure that everything is kept clean and nobody becomes ill, which is so often the case when we have a large group of men all together?"

"Well that decision is to be taken by the General, so I can not really give a realistic answer, otherwise I think you should be prepared for a long stay."

Eventually the medical orderly finished his meal and left them, muttering something about the nutrients and possible disease, which was always a concern. After the medical orderly left them Hugh and Thalius wandered back to their tent and after a while Thalius went to sleep, while Hugh lay thinking about the Jews and their extreme views, like the Zealots who were holding out in Masada and then of the other extremists, like the Christians and he remembered the large man who had been crucified upside down just outside Rome. Hugh remembered his final words about how he would not deny his saviour again, referring to when he died. Hugh did not really understand, but he wanted to know more about the Christian belief. He eventually fell asleep and was keen to see what happened at the meeting scheduled tomorrow after the midday break.

Eventually the meeting was called and all the senior officers of the three Legions were there. Eventually Hugh handed his drawings to the General, complete with his estimates about the height of the posts of Masada, including what he and Thalius had considered must be in the palace, like plenty of fresh water in the cisterns, as well as plenty of food so that the palace would have to be broken into.

The General said, "Thank you for this detailed information, Hugh, I think we must prepare ourselves for a long break, as I think it will be a long time before we can break into Masada!"

Hugh took a deep breath before saying, "I am afraid you are correct Sir, I also think that the only way to break into Masada is to follow the idea that you had of building a ramp right up to the gates, where we can manoeuvre a siege to break down the door and deal with the Zealots, by either capturing them or killing them."

"It is a shame, but I believe you are correct, Hugh and I must thank you for climbing up the cliff and making the drawings."

The rest of the meeting was spent considering how the ramp was to be made and also how the siege engine was to be constructed. There was a lot of concern first by all the three Legati, as they all said that soldiers should not do work that would normally be carried out by craftsmen assisted by slaves.

The meeting continued with the General saying, "I am not suggesting that the soldiers do all the work, but we can at least start work, it will take a long time and we can organise plenty of other things to try to keep the men happy, while all the necessary materials are gathered."

The meeting was very long and when the dinner gong sounded and the General ordered that some food be brought into his tent, so the senior officers could eat well while they discussed what had to be done. Hugh was not surprised that he was asked to work on the beginnings of the ramp. The General said, "It needs to be at an angle that allows the attacking forces to push on a siege tower on wheels, which means that the length of the ramp need to be a lot stronger, than the height. However, I am sure that we have an engineer who understands the principles of the mechanics, he must supervise the scheme." Hugh was not surprised that the meeting went on so long, because they had to discuss all sorts of things, such as activities to keep all the soldiers fully battle trained and not bored by the inactivity. These things were surprisingly varied and included chariot racing, as well as wrestling matches and mock sword fights. All of these were in addition to the normal routine that was organised whenever a legion was not in battle. Eventually the meeting finished and Hugh was pleased to return to his tent.

Hugh told Thalius all about the meeting and also how they would have to work on the ramp. "I had the feeling that we would end up working on the idea of the ramp, do you have any ideas," Thalius enquired?

"Well, yes I do. Do you remember that I made a small dam to make the water from the stream deep enough to wash all the salt deposit?" Hugh asked.

"Yes, I remember very well, but do you think it will hold together without anything to bind it together, like the mortar that they use on new buildings?" Thalius enquired.

"Well Thalius, surely you remember what I was saying about the salt which dried in the air. I was wondering if we could use that to hold all the rocks together," remarked Hugh.

"Maybe Hugh, it is certainly worth trying. We will have to try it out with the master craftsman and see what he thinks."

They considered their decision about building the ramp, until they both fell asleep, both wondering how long they would be here, without realising that they were both having the same thoughts.

Hugh was up just before sunrise, as he normally awoke fairly early, and insisted that Thalius rose as well and complete his daily exercise to keep himself very fit. As soon as they had finished breakfast in the mess, the overseer who had been appointed by the General came to see them. "Good morning Hugh and Thalius," he said almost in response to the surprised expression on Thalius's face, "I was told that you two would be here. Would you please come with me as I need to mark out where we are going to build the ramp up to the Palace of Masada."

"Have you worked out how you will build it?" enquired Hugh politely.

"I was wondering about the idea you mentioned to the general about using the drying salt crystals. You see it would save an awful lot of time and when you are already having to wait for all the materials for the siege engine that we are going to build and push up the ramp."

"Have you any idea how long the job will take?" enquired Thelius.

"No, I am afraid not," said the Overseer. "Although it is going to take a long time." They had reached the place the Overseer wanted to start, they paced out all the area and he wanted them to mark out the areas in the sand. "Use spades to dig out a shallow trench."

They had been working for quite a long time and Hugh and Thalius were beginning to feel the heat from the reflection of the bright sun in the east, when a party made up of Senator Latitch and his guards came over to ask what they were doing, temporally halting their work.

Marcus Anthony came over and said, "My men do not have to answer any questions from you, as you are being held captive by the General." Who came over as if he had realised that a problem was brewing, "It is alright Legatus, I will speak to the Senator." The General turned to face Senator Latitch and surprisingly calmly asked, "Will you please come with me Senator you may bring your bodyguards, although I will bring Hugh and Thalius, not for any other reason than to witness what is being said, because I do not trust you, as you well know." The Senator and his bodyguards went meekly after the General, with Hugh and Thalius following. The General went to his tent, where the meeting had taken place the day before and the table was still littered with drawings and diagrams. "You seem to be very interested in what we are doing," enquired the General still using a calm polite voice.

"Yes I am," squeaked the senator.

To the senator's horror and immediate recoil the general drew his sword and thrust it straight into the table were it stood quivering. "Now listen Senator, because of your stupidly sending a message back to Rome from Jerusalem, I will have to keep all three legions here to capture these damned rebels inside this damn fortress instead of a cohort of soldiers to ensure they do not escape and cause trouble. Do you realise what your stupid arrogance has cost? We do not know how long we will be here or how long it will take to break in to the Palace called Masada. If you have any suggestions I would like to hear them."

The senator gulped and then squeaked, "I think you should send some soldiers to demand that they surrender."

"These men holding out in the Palace are Zealots which means they are fanatics and they will never surrender."

"Who says they are fanatics?" asked the senator.

"This man here," replied the General indicating a small man who had been unnoticed by all the soldiers in the large tent. "He is called Jeremiah and he is one of the Jewish priests from the community that live here. I am sure he will verify my words, although I think that you must go up the cliff yourself and demand that the Zealots surrender, as you alone speak for the Emperor."

Hugh simply looked at Thalius and they both realised how the senator had walked into a trap from which he could not escape.

Hugh and Thalius returned to the Master Craftsman, who was now selecting large stones, which were being placed to form the foundation of the ramp. Over this, small stones were placed and then the whole area was washed with salt water from the Dead Sea. The Master craftsman said, "We will try the idea that you had, of binding the stones with the dried salt, although it is an unusual and untested method, but nonetheless it is worth trying. This work took nearly all that day, after which they retired to their tent, feeling very tired as it had been very hard work. When they had the evening meal in the mess, they were joined by the doctor to whom Hugh had talked about the healing powers of the Dead Sea. "Your idea seems to work with most skin conditions, and minor injuries, although the people who we have tried it on have complained that it is very painful. However as long as it works, I do not worry about complaints made by soldiers, who are just like children, even though they are supposed to be tough." After the doctor walked away Thalius look at Hugh with renewed respect.

"Well it seems that people are now listening to me," said Hugh. "It seems that people are now believing in me, so I trust you now apologise?"

"Most certainly Tribune," said Thalius jumping to his feet and saluting. "Anyway my friend what do you think the senator will do now? It was a superb way that the General trapped him."

"Thank you Thalius, yes you are right, the General really caught out Senator Latitch, I believe he is still arguing with the Priest Jeremiah and from what I overheard he is planning to take him up the cliff face tomorrow, to act as an interpreter, because the Zealots have refused to speak our language."

The next day, working with the Overseer on the constructions of the ramp, he was delighted with the way that the stones had dried with the salt binding them although it gave everything a very unusual white covering colouring so he now tried another layer of stones laid in a slightly different style, these were then covered again by more saltwater. Surprisingly the original layer of stones did not weaken when they were doused with more saltwater. Eventually, after they had added a lot more stones, Hugh asked, "Have you any idea of how long it will take Sir?"

The Overseer replied, "Not really, you see one of the problems is that each layer of stones will have to be brought from further away, so I cannot really give any accurate estimate. He then added as an afterthought, "The other problem of course is the siege tower, which has to be sturdy but light enough to be pushed up the ramp. The senior woodcraftsman from another legion is working on that, but again all the wood will have to come from Jerusalem or further up in Judea."

Thalius said to Hugh. "I believe you said that there would be a meeting tonight, so you may have an idea, because I think all the soldiers are beginning to wonder how long this job will take."

"Obviously I'll try to find out what is happening. I myself am beginning to wonder how long we will be here."

At the meeting that evening Hugh heard Legatus Marcus Anthony ask the General, "I really have no idea Lagatus, but as you know I have asked one of the other legions to a series of competitions that will hopefully keep the men interested and competitive. So we will just have to wait and see if the senator's plea to the Zealots will have any effect in getting them out of Masada." He shrugged indicating his apology to all the senior officers. It was quite an interesting meeting from then on as many ideas were put forward for activities to keep morale from flagging. Hugh felt quite interested in some of the competitions like wrestling and mock gladiator type fights, where no sharp weapons would be used. The meeting was not very long, although many people left with a better frame of mind than that expected.

When Hugh returned to his tent and Thalius, he explained about the events that would be planned.

"I think we should try out for the wrestling and the chariot racing, I bet I could beat you in the wrestling."

"Oh yes, you and who else?" replied Hugh scornfully. Hugh then told him about the senator taking Jeremiah as an interpreter up to the place where they had made their detailed map of the palace.

"I cannot imagine anything the senator says will make any difference, what do you think Hugh?" Hugh simply shrugged, with a sort of, 'we will just wait and see', expression.

They continued to chat about many of the events that were being organised, to keep the soldiers from becoming bored.

They both realised it would be difficult with approximately sixteen thousand men and one fairly small area.

They were on their way to where they had been working on the ramp, when the General called them. "I would like you to accompany the senator and his bodyguards. He then spoke very quietly so that only Hugh and Thalius could hear him, "Make sure you watch the palace, because I feel sure that the senator's demands may result in some form of retaliation." Hugh gave a nod to indicate that he understood and walked over to where the senator was waiting.

"Would you like to follow us Senator, you see it was myself and Centurion Thalius who made the climb up the rock face." The senator seemed that he was about to reply, but he decided not to and simple followed them to the bottom of the cliff. Hugh was about to begin the climb, which he knew very well although Thalius checked him with a brief touch. The senator seemed to be arguing with the bodyguards, his voice rose until he was almost screaming at his men.

"You will have to carry me on a chair." And then the bodyguards rushed to find a suitable chair that they could manage to fasten to two carrying poles.

"Why do you think that he is demanding to be carried?" said Thalius.

"Obvious really," replied Hugh, "he has legs like twigs, apart from which it makes him look more important." So the climb was eventfully started, with Hugh and Thalius being follow by the senator's bodyguards carrying the senator on a chair.

The climb seemed to take even longer than twice the time that Hugh and Thalius had previously taken, because the bodyguards carrying the Senator had a lot of difficulty, particularly in keeping the Senator's chair level. Senator Latitch kept shouting and yelling at them, if they made him uncomfortable, so the climb was extremely tedious and Hugh actually felt sorry for the bodyguards, even though they had tried to kill him once back on Mount Vesuvius. The sweating bodyguards were followed by the small Jewish priest, who had the job of acting as an interpreter, he was remarkably nimble and Hugh realised that he had probably climbed up the rock face quite a few times himself. Eventually they reached the place where Hugh and Thalius had sat and made their drawings and they actually helped the bodyguards to secure the chair to the rock face by using the rope that Hugh and Thalius had left attached to the rock outcrop. The Senator had a speaking trumpet as used between galleys on the sea and this he put to his lips and called out, "I am one of the Roman Empire's leading senators, I speak to you directly from the Emperor of the Roman Empire." His words were then shouted by the Priest who had a remarkably powerful voice. At first there seemed to be nothing happening at the palace, but then the door began to open slowly and a large machine was revealed that they did not recognise until Hugh realised that it was some form of a catapult and a shower of small stones were sent whistling towards them. Hugh and Thalius ducked, as did the Priest, yet some of the stones still hit them. However the senator and his men were directly in line and it was not only stone that were thrown, but also a heavy javelin which hit the senator right in the middle of his chest and passed right through him until it came out between his shoulder blades, complete with a stream of blood. The Senator's chair was thrown back and the senator screamed as he fell down the cliff face, where he landed at the general's feet, obviously completely dead. The palace doors were closed and the party made their descent of the cliff face to where the General stood looking at the bloody remains of the senator.

"Well at least I can now send a message back to Rome, so we now know what we knew all along," he said as he prodded the mangled remains of Senator Latitch. Hugh could not be sure, but he felt the General was pleased as he smiled briefly at him.

Epilogue

Breakthrough

The Senator's body was cremated by the Dead Sea, the ashes were sent back all the way to Rome with a scroll from the General, which was witnessed by the three Legatos it took the best part of three years to build the ramp, although the work had been started by soldiers, there was now a slight delay before builders were brought in from Jerusalem and Jerico. The Legions started to enjoy their stay by the Dead Sea, enjoying all the activities that had been planned. However the ramp and the siege engine were finally completed and they were hauled up to Masada. But it took a long time to haul and push the siege engine into place. Now when the final assault was made and the breech was made into the Palace, they discovered nothing but dead bodies, as all the Zealots had committed suicide by falling on their own swords.

All three legions eventually broke their camp and returned to Rome, to be sent to other areas of the Roman Empire. Although General Priam retired from his long and dedicated service, although he was not noted in any records.

Author's Notes

The characters in this story are fictional although it is a story that is a story that is based on fact. The 9th Legion did exist and was lost in Britain, possibly by Queen Boadicea, who was a very savage Queen from the north of Britain, who hoped to drive the Romans from this green and pleasant land.

I have used the name of a General, which is probably incorrect, although there must have been one leader of the three legions for the campaign against Masada. If you visit the site, you can either climb the cliff by the path, or you can take the cable car, as I have done on my visits to Israel. Israel includes Judea that was a separate state to Galilee in the north, where Jesus Christ came from, although we are fairly sure he was born in Bethlehem but returned with his parents to Nazareth where he grew up and began his career as a carpenter, before pursuing his belief, but you must recall that he never claimed to be the son of god.

His family came from Nazareth and he started his teaching in Galilee, probably using St Peter house in Capernaum. All his disciples were originally fisherman, who fished in fresh water lake that ran down into Galilee.

The Jews were dispersed by the revolt in Jerusalem and that was the cause of what is called the Diaspora. When the Jews left Judea and spread all over the world, a couple of settlements remained in Galilee, like the settlement at Safad.

Glossary of Characters

Arte	Ox wagon driver
Adobe	The Negro Gladiator
Aurolius	Owner of the Gladiators
Boadicea	Queen of the Iceni people
Brutaus	The captain of the Senator Latitch's galley
Crelux	Centurion in charge of training new soldiers
Cynthia	General Priam's sister
General Priam	The General who captured Hugh
Gildar	A fellow trainee soldier
Hugh	British Gladiator
Lydia	A soldier's wife who became friendly with Rosanna
Marcus	A soldier in the same cohort as Hugh
Petros	Hugh and Rosanna's first son
Rolex	Centurion in charge of Hugh's cohort
Rosanna	Hugh's wife
Senator Latitch	Senator from Rome
Timothy	A soldier in the same cohort as Hugh
Harot	A tribune Hugh met in Gibraltar
Thalius	Slave 97 freed by Hugh on board the galley
Titonia	Thalius girlfriend taken away from him
Zacceus	Important Merchant from Judea
Yahweh	God of the Jewish people
Marcus Anthony	Leader of the 3rd legion
Salerno	Scene of the uprising led by Spartacus
Spartacus	Leader of the uprising at Salerno
Kreol	Centurion drives Hugh's chariot to Salerno
Jeremiah	Jewish priests from the community that live near Masada